HOMESTEAD

HOMESTEAD

Rosina Lippi

Delphinium Books

Harrison, New York   Encino, California

"Laura" originally appeared in slightly different form as "What Laura Wanted," *Epoch*, vol. 32, no. 1 (1994). "Mikatrin" originally appeared in slightly different form as "Katy Marie–1943," *Glimmer Train Stories* (Spring 1994).

Library of Congress Cataloging-in-Publication Data

Lippi, Rosina, 1956-

Homestead / Rosina Lippi. – 1st ed.

p.   cm.

ISBN 1-883285-14-3 (acid-free paper)

I.Title.

PS3562.I5795H65 1998

813'.54–dc21   97-35269

CIP

First Edition

10 9 8 7 6 5 4 3 2 1

Distributed by HarperCollins Publishers

Printed in the United States of America on acid-free paper

Designed by Krystyna Skalski

For Marlies, who shows me how to be a mother

For Elisabeth, who makes a mother of me

Vergealt's Gott

Contents

We write not to be understood, we write to understand.

Cecil Day-Lewis

Author's Note

Rosenau, the setting of *Homestead*, is an amalgam of many of the villages of the Bregenz Forest in Vorarlberg, Austria's western most province. It lies at an altitude and in a topographical setting similar to that of Damüls or Schröcken; it is as isolated as Sibratsgfäll or the alps at Schönebach; its church can be found in Hirschau or Großdorf; its church square might be the one in Andelsbuch or Hittisau; its farmhouses are scattered throughout the villages from Egg to Schoppernau.

In the almost four years I lived and worked in the Bregenz Forest, first going to college and teaching, then collecting data for a study of the incredibly beautiful and challenging dialect spoken there, I spent many hours talking to women of all ages, particularly in the villages of Andelsbuch, Egg, and primarily Großdorf. While I was listening to their vowels, they were teaching me what it means to be a storyteller. These women, I am sure, will sometimes see glimpses of themselves here, but no one character is meant as, or should be construed as being, any real person. In the end, this is a work of fiction.

Anna

Bengat Homestead 1909

"Man Proposes GOD Disposes," read the faded proclamation painted across the shingles above the Wainwright's door. With those stern words over her head, Anna of Bengat homestead stood hesitating on the stone steps that led to the village shop. Beside her was her nephew Stante; at her back and all around was a near perfect circle of mountains.

The Wainwright's homestead took up a good portion of the center of Rosenau, sprawling along the square across from the church, the Golden Eagle, and Goat-Cheese Willi's tidy homestead. Long ago the house had been painted with steer's blood in the old fashion, but now the shingled walls were a flaking, clotted reddish brown. Down the west side of the house ran the long passageway of the *Schopf*, an enclosed two-story gallery of silver-gray wood; it was piled high with feed sacks leaking pale streams of oats. A heap of wagon wheels awaiting repair erupted from the workshop into the dirt road.

At the far end of the building where the house melded into cowshed and barn, a speckled hen pecked despondently around a manure heap so old and high that even the flies had tired of it. A procession of sunflowers with hunched shoulders and drooping heads stretched out into the pasture toward God's Acre.

Stante tugged at Anna's sleeve. She took his hand and together they went into the shop, which smelled of vinegar and axle grease and cinnamon. Here the Wainwright's spinster daughter waited on customers every morning with cold efficiency and a notable lack of goodwill. Her father might run a slovenly farmstead, but the household and the shop were Grumpy Marie's domain, and she kept them as clean and stern as she kept herself. In exchange for cloth, ribbons, buttons, hairpins, thread and needles, lye, whetstones, penny nails, tin buckets, mustache wax, nail clippers, tobacco, paper stock, ink, horse tonic, cooking pots and pottery, coffee beans and tea leaves, brown and white sugar, salt, spices, feed cake and three grades of cornmeal, Grumpy Marie took in coins, gossip, surplus eggs, and an occasional bottle of homemade schnapps or crock of honey. On Mondays and Thursdays Marie was less surly, for on those mornings it fell to her to sort the mail that came up from Ackenau with the courier. When snow closed the road and kept the courier away, folks kept clear of the shop and Marie as long as they could.

On this particular Monday morning in early July, Anna was surprised to see Marie perched high on a box in the middle of the dim room, surrounded by a crowd of women. Small and lean, she was flushed with high color, and her mood put a hum in the air. What business she could have with these women— all ages, from all over the village—on a workday morning, Anna could not imagine. But she had been called, and she had come.

"Finally," Marie said when she caught sight of Anna. "Took long enough. Now we can get started." She fixed Stante with a stare and gestured over her shoulder with a toss of her head. "Go look after your brother."

The boy glanced quickly at Anna and scooted out the door.

Marie worked her jaw silently and looked around the circle of women as if there were marks on their foreheads only she could see. They looked back at her, perplexed but curious enough to bide a while.

"You all sign your names Anna Fink," she stated.

"A-yo," Gide's Annakatrin agreed in a long drawl. "I guess that's true enough. Every one of us baptized an Anna-something-or-other, and a Fink too."

"Half the folks in the village sign themselves Fink," added Annobüobli's Anna, sixteen and easily bored. "Did you haul us all down here to tell us our names?"

Marie's stare was enough to make the girl fluster and drop her gaze. She said, "Today the courier brought a picture postcard, addressed to Anna Fink."

There was a hesitation as the women looked at each other.

"That postcard can't be for me," Anna said, confused. "Peter took me home to Bengat ten years ago, and I've been signing myself Sutterlüty ever since."

Marie shrugged. "You belonged to Jodok Fink of River's Bend before you married Bengato Peter. And I got a card here addressed to Anna Fink, which I am obliged to deliver, or return."

"Well, ain't there no housename on the thing?" asked Annimi, her gaze wandering over the bolts of calico and muslin.

With a withering look, Marie reached into her apron pocket and withdrew the postcard. Watery blues and greens glinted between her muscular fingers. "'Anna Fink,'" she read. "'At the River's Bend, Rosenau.'"

They turned together to look at Bengato Peter's Anna.

"It's been ten years!" she repeated, squirming slightly.

"But you were Anna Fink before that," said Annakatrin. "No Fink women ever lived down to the River's Bend homestead except you and Rosa."

"Ten years is a long time, though," conceded Pitchfork Paulus's Annatheres thoughtfully.

"Well, there's an easier way," said Fellele's Annele. She alternated her weight clumsily from one foot to the other, trying to shift the burden of a nine-month pregnancy from the small of her back. "Who's it from, Marie?"

"I don't read the mail!"

"Course you don't," said Annimi, too smoothly. "Give it over to us and we'll sort it out amongst ourselves."

"Never mind that," Marie snapped, jerking the card up and away as if Annimi had snatched at it. "I got a feeling this has to do with you," she said, turning to Anna. "No matter how long you been up at Bengat."

"Well, all I know is, I'm eighty this past Maundy Tuesday, and I have never got a picture postcard in the mail," Annakatrin said, shaking her head. "Don't know who'd send me one."

"Then you take it, Annakatrin," said Anna, frustrated now.

But Marie grunted and thrust the card toward her. The simpleness of the gesture was disarming, and Anna, who had just told herself that she had no intention of taking it, found the postcard in her hand.

"There's a mistake," Marie said with grim satisfaction, hovering as if Anna were a stranger from the flatlands and Marie had just been obliged to put a newborn into her arms, against all good judgment. "You'll see."

Anna fingered the thick card stock. She saw a fine drawing of an imposing building, lawns running down to a pier, people strolling, sailboats scattered on blue waves, Lake Constance as smooth and clear as expensive paper could render it. "The White Horse Hotel" stood in sloping letters across the bottom, and: "For the discerning traveler."

"Get on with it!" Marie said, so Anna turned the card over and read out loud, the book language filling her mouth with its sparseness. It had always reminded her of unripe fruit, resistant and without flavor, something unnatural and of little use or beauty.

"'Dear Anna,'" she read. "'It has been so long. Please forgive me. I never meant it to be so long. Please have patience. Your Anton. P.S. Please write to me here, I am very lonely.'"

There was a small silence.

"Look at those boats. How many folks you think can ride in one of those?"

"Anton. We got enough of them around here, but don't suppose this is one of ours."

"He writes pretty."

"What does 'P.S.' mean?"

"It means 'I ain't done yet.'"

"Where is that place?"

"Never seen the lake myself, except from the northmost ridge of the Third Sister on a clear day."

"Why's that woman carrying a rain-roof in the bright sunlight?"

"That's no rain-roof, you ijit. That's called a parasol. Keeps the sun off her white skin." This from Annatheres, who had inherited from her mother, a flatlander, three copies of the *Ladies Afternoon Journal:* January 1891, February 1895, and the general favorite in the village, July 1900. Annatheres had committed most of all three to memory, and could hold forth on articles of clothing of strange construction and dubious utility.

"What does 'discerning' mean then, if you're so smart?"

"Rich," said Annatheres. "Sticky rich."

Anna never looked up from the card. She saw that this man with the same name as her youngest boy, this man who stayed at expensive hotels and wrote in an elegant hand (Anna had never seen the like, not even from Father Meusburger, who had taught her her letters), had written "please" three times in five short sentences. She wondered how disappointed he would be when he had no reply from his Anna.

Marie stuck out her hand. "I'll send it back where it came from," she said in a tone that allowed no disagreement, but Annakatrin stepped in.

"Marie, you would have made a fine nun. You got the knack."

"The tongue, too," muttered Annatheres.

"There's business needs looking after," Marie said hotly.

"We're looking after it, ain't we? Now let Anna have her say."

"It's mine," Anna said, surprising herself as much as she did Grumpy Marie. She put the card in her basket, and with that she went outside and walked toward the public well in the center of the church square. Anna sat down on the edge of the horse trough with the postcard in her lap.

Marie stood in the doorway, hands on her hips, and watched as the others trailed out after Anna.

With considerable shifting and nudging they managed to balance seven abreast on the edge of the trough, seven blue work aprons over pleated black linen skirts, once glassy with starch but now softened and wilting, like crackled sugar glaze. Below the skirts, seven sets of dusty bare feet peeked out. Without comment, Anna passed the card to her right, and one by one each of the Annas claimed it. Each read it slowly, ran a fingertip over the cool surface, spelled out the mysterious abbreviations on the stamp and the cancellation. Broommaker's Annamarile, who had not dared say a word in front of Grumpy Marie, let out an audible sigh when she got up to hand it back, finally, to Anna.

The church bell rang nine, and they startled at the morning half gone. In a flurry of skirts they were up and headed for home.

Anna got up to go too but froze when Annakatrin turned back from across the square and hollered, "You best write and tell the man he's gone wrong!"

Halfway home to Bengat, Anna stopped and retrieved the card: the blue-green waters, the little pier, the grass that stretched in a cool sheet down to the shore. A gentleman with a walking stick. A lady in white linen, wearing long gloves and carrying a parasol, her hair rolled elaborately on the back of her head. Anna touched the braids wrapped around her own head.

She was about to set out again when she caught a flash of color: Stante, bolting straight up the lower hang of the Second Sister as if the devil were close behind. She watched him climb the hang like a ladder, ignoring the dirt path and its switchbacks. The July sun shone like a cap on his head.

He came to a sudden halt just before her and smiled, not even short of breath.

"What is it?" Anna asked. "Did Marie send you chasing after me?"

His blue eyes were striking for their contrast to his sun-browned skin, and for their perpetual look of confusion. Anna watched Stante try to find the words he wanted, and fail. As she often did, she found herself wishing that she could give this child, her dead sister's boy, what God had seen fit to hold back: the ability to open his mouth and say what was on his mind. For a moment Anna was tempted to sit down right where she was and take him into her lap and rock him.

"Were you wanting to come visit up at Bengat?"

The flash of excitement in Stante's eyes told her that she had guessed why he'd come after her. The way he dropped his gaze told her that he had come without permission.

It was so rare that the Wainwright let Stante or Michel come up to Bengat. He put little value on the twins, but neither would he let them go. Every year on their birthday—the anniversary of her sister's death–Anna asked once again if she could take the boys in and see to their raising; every year the Wainwright turned her down.

"You best be getting back," Anna said softly. "But you come up again soon and bring Michel with you. In the wheelbarrow. You think you can push your brother all the way up to Bengat for some plum dumplings?"

Stante grinned at her and nodded.

"But next time come by the road," she said, laughing. Anna rubbed her palm over the crown of his head, and he turned and preened like a cat under her touch.

The men were most taken by the lawn. Their lives were ruled by a simple cycle: they needed milk from the cows to make cheese, the cows needed grass to produce milk, the grass needed cow dung to grow. Peter and his father could not understand grass without a purpose, without animals.

"Maybe they graze goats in the night," suggested Anna's mother-in-law, Isabella.

But they looked silently at the lawn, smooth as a silk handkerchief, and put no real credence in that idea.

"So you'll write an answer," Alois said. Her father-in-law was a reasonable man, but not one disposed to long discussion.

"If you think so–" Anna glanced at Peter, who nodded.

"Imagine the man," said Peter's sister, Barbara. "Waiting and waiting on a word from her, from this Anna. Whoever she is."

"I'll write it for you, Mama," Olga volunteered. At nine she was Anna's oldest, more interested in schoolwork than taking care of two little brothers, and proud of her handwriting.

"It's your mama's business," Peter said gently.

Alois gave Anna his fountain pen and showed her how to fill the barrel. Her sister-in-law cut edges and blank spots out of the *Farmer's Weekly* for Anna to practice on. Olga sharpened the pencil with Alois's penknife, under Isabella's careful eye.

Only Peter seemed content to let Anna get on with it in her own time, but even that didn't last.

"There's a Rosenau over on the other side of Innsbruck, I seem to recall," Peter said when he climbed into bed that night. "Maybe you could say so."

"You don't mind me writing to this stranger?"

"Don't suppose you could fall in love with a man on the strength of his handwriting," said Peter, yawning. Then he fell asleep, as he always did, without warning.

Lying next to him, drowsy but strangely content to be awake, Anna realized that she had no clear memory of Peter's handwriting, having seen it so few times in her life. He had finished his four years of schooling before she began her own; when she married him, she had never once seen him with a pen in his hand. Then Anna remembered the marriage registry and Peter's signature, uneven and awkward. She put the thought away and reached for sleep.

The next afternoon, when Isabella and Barbara took Olga off to Lost Calf Meadow to rake hay, Anna settled her two boys down to nap. Then she put a clean blue bibbed apron over her workday *Juppa*, crossing the wide starched strings neatly over her back, winding them around her waist, and tying the ends into a bow at the base of her spine. Out of habit she put her marketing basket over her arm and went down to the village to buy a postcard. On the way she was stopped three times by folks who wanted to see the picture of the fine hotel and were disappointed that she had left it behind.

"There's a village called Rosanna way over in the Pustertal," Goat-Cheese Willi called to her across his dung heap. The innkeeper came out of the Golden Eagle to tell her the same thing.

Stepping from sunlight into the pungent shadows of the shop, Anna heard the Wainwright before she saw him.

"Woolly-woolly," he was crooning softly in his crackly old man's voice. "Woolly-head."

Stante stood red-faced next to his grandfather. The Wainwright was wobbling the boy's head back and forth with a shovel-like hand. He looked up at Anna as she came in, and stopped. It wasn't her disapproval that worried him, Anna knew that: he was just tired of the game.

With a forced nod to the Wainwright, Anna addressed her first words to Stante, and was rewarded immediately with his smile. There was a scuffling in the far corner of the room, and that is where Anna found Michel, tied with a shank of rope to a foot of the tiled oven.

"He will run off," the Wainwright said to Anna's back. "Can't keep track of him otherwise. The Lord knows what devilment he'd get up to."

Where Stante seemed incapable of expecting anything from Anna that wasn't soft and soothing, Michel could only look at her with hooded eyes. She crouched down next to him and reached out; Michel tolerated her caress. Anna was surprised once again, as she always was when she saw him, at how much of her sister she could find in his face.

"It's been a while since you come up to see us, Michel," Anna said, and he looked at her hopefully. "We'll see what we can do," she whispered.

Rosa had died before she knew about Stante, who had his mother's beauty but nothing else to call his own; or about Michel, whose mind was whole but whose body was frail and bird-like, the bones bent into unlikely angles at all the wrong spots. Stante could barely put a sentence together; Michel had a clear high voice and a head full of things to say, but he seldom chose to speak. Rosa had died and left these boys to her husband; her husband had taken the influenza and died the year after, leaving the boys not to Anna, who wanted to take them in, but to his father, the Wainwright.

"Your sister," said the Wainwright behind Anna, as if that explained everything away, Stante's tears, the rope burns on Michel's ankle.

Anna straightened up and lifted an eyebrow, her face stiff with anger. "My sister?"

"How'd she manage it, I often wonder. Two half boys instead of a whole one."

"These children are welcome at Bengat," Anna said, her words feeling tight and small and insufficient.

"They are my only grandsons, sorry as they may be. Nobody will ever say I ain't done my duty by these two since my Richard passed on. Woolly here may never be the craftsman his daddy was, but he is a good hand in the toolshop when he keeps his few wits about him, ain't you, Woolly?"

"Where is it?" Marie said from the doorway, and both Anna and the Wainwright turned in surprise. "Did you bring it back?"

Anna looked from her nephews to Marie.

"Did you bring the picture postcard back?" Marie said again, flapping her apron.

"I'd like a penny postcard," Anna said.

Marie drew up. "So you are fixing to write."

Anna put a coin on the counter.

"I'd like a postcard," she repeated.

"That's all you got to say?"

"And a stamp."

The Wainwright held up a hand to cut Marie off. "Let me ask you this," he said as he put the postcard on the counter in front of Anna. "When's the last time you spoke the book language?"

Confused by this question, Anna dropped her eyes from his toothy smile.

"Bet you haven't spoke the book language in years. Couldn't write book-like any more than you could write Greek."

"I'm the postmistress," Marie said with a withering look

at her father, who had clearly missed the point. "It is my responsibility."

Anna turned away from them, from their sourness and grim self-righteousness, and left without another word to her nephews.

"Could have been any one of you Finka-Annas!" Marie called after her. "Or none of you!"

Anna forced herself to walk at a steady pace through the square, although she could feel their gaze on her back, hot and demanding as the July sun: Stante's eyes like dusty windows, willing her to turn around because he loved her; Marie's eyes, narrowed and flickering with irritation because she had let Anna get the upper hand and hadn't yet figured out how to put things right.

That evening Anna was distracted; she stoked the stove thoughtlessly and the milk billowed up and over; she snapped at Olga and then made the boys sit still so she could cut their hair. At just over one, Tony had little to cut, and she was quickly finished with him, but Anna made Jos wait too long, fussing at the job when it was clear that the boy just wanted to be up and gone. Barbara pressed her lips together hard and left the kitchen, but Isabella gave her a penetrating look, her brown eyes all the sharper in the soft roundness of her face. Anna looked away, and counted on the fact that her mother-in-law was the sort who kept her opinion to herself.

Later, by lamplight, Anna sat alone at the table in the *Stube* with her things gathered round her: the blank card propped up against the oil lamp, the fountain pen in its stand, the pile of scrap paper. She took a pencil and wrote "Dear Sir," and then: "Your postcard came to me."

Anna felt her fingers cramping on the pencil; a fine line of sweat broke out on her brow. Suddenly she wondered why she had taken the card from Marie, what she had meant by it.

She turned it over to read it again, and again she counted: he had written "please" three times. Knowing she was being unfair, knowing herself fortunate in marriage, Anna tried to remember the last time Peter had asked her with "please." She forced her mind back over old conversations, days and weeks old, with increasing disquiet. The truth was, Peter didn't use the word much, but then he had such a gentle way about him that it had never occurred to her before to feel a lack. This stranger, this Anton, he was a different kind of creature from Peter; even in those few lines she could feel it. Anna picked up the pencil again, and tried to put down what she thought he would need to know.

I grew up on the River's Bend homestead in Rosenau. That was some years ago, afore my folks passed on and my sister Rosa and her husband took over and I married away, up the mountain side. The house there has stood empty since Rosa and her husband died. The hayfields are pacted out now. I live at Bengat with my husband and his folks and my own children. I am a farmer's wife and nothing more. Your card is very beautiful, but it does not belong to me.

Anna looked at these words for some time, and it seemed to her she could hear Father Meusburger standing behind her, his fingers rasping softly in the folds of his cassock. She was suffused with the same compressed dread she had felt in the schoolroom of the little rectory, where she hunched over her square of chalk tablet, copying out catechism sentences written on the board in the priest's sharp-edged hand. The book language was a strange maze, but she saw now she could find her way through it, if she moved slowly, and if she felt her way carefully along the barren walls, and most important, if she could be content with half-truths. The pencil was heavy in her hand, and it found the paper again. What came from it surprised her, but she let it flow.

> *Once a young man came through Rosenau on a mountain tour. He was tall and his skin was the color of old honey. His eyes shiny black like his hair. He talked strange, bookish but not bookish, putting his sentences round backwards at times. He stayed in our barn for some days. He ate with us, and paid Daddy good coin. Our Rosa was taken with him. She would sit at the window and watch him come down the road. That was before she married Wainwright's Richard, before her twins came along. Rosa died in childbed.*

When Anna went upstairs, Peter was asleep. She undressed slowly without the lamp so as not to disturb him. Then she got into bed and shook him awake.

"Those boys are my flesh and blood, and I want them here," she told her husband, her voice hard and full, and then she let Peter hold her instead of saying all the things she already knew but didn't want to hear, instead of making her empty promises about children she could not claim, but to whom she was bound by guilt and love.

The next evening Anna worked over her postcard while the family sat together out in the *Schopf* with the wooden shutters folded and propped up to let in the evening breeze. The newspaper scraps Barbara had cut out for her were soon gone, so with a furtive look out the window Anna took three sheets of yellowing stationery from her father-in-law's oaken lap desk and hoped it would be enough. She wrote in pencil, in a hand that was small and cramped but became looser, more generous, more complex with every line. In time she didn't have to wait for the words to come to her in the book language; it was as if she had opened some creaky gate that now swung smooth.

At first she wrote about her sister and her sister's boys, about Michel's egg-like skull that seemed to twist sideways on his neck as if his ear were attached to the shoulder, so you could never know what he was looking at. She wrote about Stante's blue eyes. Anna took more paper and wrote about how Peter first came courting, about her father-in-law's habit of whistling to the barn swallows and how they seemed to listen.

She forgot she was writing to a stranger, a man she had never seen: she imagined him love-struck, lonely, wearing a white linen suit and silk hat and smoking a carved pipe under the striped awnings of the the White Horse Hotel. Slowly this image faded away into the paper under her hands until she could see much less of him than she could of herself, as a young girl, a bride, a mother, an aunt.

When she had used all the stationery in the lap desk, ten sheets, Anna looked up with a start and saw it was near midnight. She folded all the newsprint and paper into one packet and tied it up with string. Then she took the blank postcard and the pen, and in quick, easy strokes she wrote out the address on one side.

> *TO: Anton, a guest of the Hotel*
> *Who Wrote to Anna at River's Bend, Rosenau*
> *The White Horse Hotel*
> *Lake Constance*

On the other side she wrote "Dear Sir," and then, with little hesitation:

> *Your card came to me by mistake. I do not know*
> *you. There is no other Anna here in Rosenau who*

lives at the River's Bend, as I did before I married. If you have not heard from your Anna, perhaps it is because she never received your card. I wish you well.

Sincerely,
Anna Sutterlüty born Fink
Bengat Homestead
Lower Hang of the Second Sister

On her way up to bed Anna stopped to check on Olga and then went into the boys' room. Tony had crept under his blanket; she tugged him back into place and smoothed his damp hair away from his face. Jos had managed to wiggle out of his nightclothes, as he always did, and he lay naked on top of his blanket. Anna admired the sheen of the moonlight on his skin even as she covered him. Sitting on the edge of Jos's bed, Anna listened to her boys breathing in counterpoint, and she wondered, as she had first done when Olga was born and as she had every day since, what she would do if the next breath didn't come, if her children were to slip away from her against her will, and refuse to return.

Peter was awake and waiting for her.

"It's a good thing we already got a Tony of our own," he said, folding back the covers.

Anna raised an eyebrow at his playful tone. "How so?"

"Because we could never baptize an Anton now without the whole village wondering what we been up to."

She laughed. "What I been up to, you mean." With her back turned to Peter she slipped her buttoned nightdress over her head. "You jealous?"

"Don't know, exactly," Peter said, reaching out to catch her wrist and pull her into bed. "You finished writing?"

She nodded.

"Then I'm not jealous." He paused. "Just what did you say?"

Anna rubbed her hand across her husband's cheek. "Want to read it?"

Peter grinned. "I'm not much of a reading man."

"Might find it interesting," Anna whispered.

"There are more interesting things in life," he said, reaching for her buttons.

"You counting on another baptism?" she asked, and this caused him to look up from her nightdress to her face.

"Why, I suppose we could manage to accommodate a few more at our table," Peter said slowly.

I have never seen Michel smile at anyone but his brother, Anna had written.

"Children need more than food," she said against Peter's hair; then, feeling the warmth of his silence and his attention, she closed her eyes.

The next morning Anna handed Grumpy Marie the card and watched her read it right there, mouthing the words one by one. Anna looked away. Neither Stante nor Michel was anywhere to be seen.

"That'll be the end of that," Marie said, and Anna was struck not by Marie's ridicule or disdain but instead by the regret in her voice. Marie was the only woman on this homestead, with animals, the wagonsmithy, the shop, two burdensome boys, and a contentious and aging father to look after; Anna was not surprised to see white in Marie's hair at less than thirty, or the weariness that hunched her back. But she was startled deep down by this glimpse of a loneliness she had never considered. Anna felt a surge of compassion and sadness for this woman, and for a moment she wished she had left the whole business to Marie, who was looking at her now with glittering eyes.

"I do my best," she said. "I do my best for those boys. They want for nothing."

Anna turned away, knowing this for the truth, but finding little comfort in it.

That afternoon Anna was sitting in the *Schopf* with the mending in her lap while Jos and Tony played in the dooryard. It was overcast and threatening rain, but they had gotten the hay into the barn before breakfast and hadn't mowed any more in the meantime. Every so often Anna felt the outline of the folded pages still in her apron pocket as she tracked the storm, approaching in fits and starts like a moody and untrustworthy lover.

The narrow road and the path that fell steeply away from it to the house were hidden from the *Schopf*, which looked down into the garden and over the village; it was a while before Anna realized that somebody was coming. She was just putting her mending aside when the first scream came, clear and shrill. The boys looked up from their play with round, blank stares; they had been brought up on the screams of pigs, goats, and cows under the knife, but this was something different. Anna leapt the stairs and rounded the corner to see Stante come flying down the road toward them, pushing Michel in a rickety wheelbarrow at a dead run over the hard-packed earth, his face transformed with joy. From inside the wheelbarrow Michel bellowed an odd, deep laughter, his mouth gaping wide, his milky skin flushed with color. Like fragile folded wings, his hands clutched at the sides of the wheelbarrow as it bounced and rattled.

Anna saw Isabella leaning out of a window, and then Alois stepped out of the barn with a wrench in his hands. Olga, caught in Stante's path with a bag of feed on her back, jumped out of the way as they sped past, and then stood staring longingly after them. Peter, his arms white with curd, had come out

of the creamery. He leaned there against the wall, his chin lowered to his chest while he laughed, laughter honest and clean,
a boy's laughter.

They watched as Stante raced his brother toward the
house, faster and faster, breathing hard, pushing with all the
strength in his legs and arms and back, while Michel rolled
in the wheelbarrow, beating with his heels, his head turned
against his shoulder, laughing and shouting up into the
summer sky.

Johanna
Bent Elbow Homestead 1916

One morning at the juncture of an early spring and an over-
eager summer, two old men idled on the doorstep of the Bengat
homestead creamery long after their business was done. They
stopped, in spite of a full day's work waiting ahead, because the
sound of cowbells on the move had been drifting down off the
slope of the Second Sister for some time. They stood quietly and
listened, the shorter of them bent over, his leathery elbows sup-
ported on the wooden crossbar of his pushcart, the other with
his head inclined.

"Bent Elbow," said Bengat's Alois, shuffling a heavy wooden
clog in the gravel.

The Wainwright grunted. He knew that Alois's hearing
and judgment were more reliable than his own; he was, after
all, only a part-time farmer with a solitary cow. Moreover, Alois
made good strong cheese, of which the Wainwright was overly
fond. He looked at the wheel he had just bought, wrapped in

cloth and nestled in his pushcart. There was a demand for Bengat dairy cheese. Nevertheless, the Wainwright found that he could not, on principle, let an opinion go unchallenged. He rubbed his shapeless blue cap over the high crown of his head and considered.

"Half-Moon Hollow," he countered just as Johanna of Bent Elbow homestead and her sister Angelika came into view on the path, driving before them two milch cows. Angelika led the horse with her daughter Mikatrin strapped into a basket-rigged sidesaddle. On Nero's far side a tower of household plunder swayed gently.

Johanna walked ahead of Nero, setting a quick but uneven pace that made her sun hat bump against her back; her cane sent small clods of dark earth flying with each step. Angelika came along behind, and while she did not limp as her sister did, there was little of grace in her step, and quite a bit of weariness.

"A-yo," Alois drawled. "Bent Elbow."

The Wainwright nodded sourly toward the bigger of the cows, an especially fine animal: deep brown in coloring, broad-backed, with a ponderous udder. "That Jupiter rolls to the left," he pointed out. Then, with a little half-smile that revealed a row of haphazardly scattered teeth, "Not that Johanna would mind."

Alois set his jaw. "A milker as generous as that one can walk any damn way she pleases."

"You may be right," said the Wainwright grudgingly. "In the case of the cow. But that Johanna's got an edge to her."

Above them, indifferent clouds in a glassy sky promised heat and a long stretch of haying weather. Alois concentrated on the feel of the breeze so as to keep his irritation from getting the upper hand. From the corner of his eye he observed the Wainwright.

Then Alois looked at Johanna, a proud, lithe woman in

spite of her hip; he had always thought a lot of her. He had hoped, once upon a time, that his son might see her for what she was and pay her some attention, but that had come to nothing. And now Peter was somewhere in Galicia, where the fighting was heating up as fast as the summer, and his Anna watched for mail with vacant eyes, sullen in her worry, short with the children.

"You'd be glad to make room for Johanna on your place if you was on your way to the Front," Alois said in spite of his resolution to keep still.

A broad smile from the Wainwright. "I'm not disputing that. Not a bit. Nope, Hans drove a good bargain when he married Angelika, got the better worker into the bargain anyway." Congratulating himself liberally on his own wit, he spun his line of reasoning out. "A-yo. I suppose those girls have to be taken as a team. Johanna to nip at you a little once in a while, keep things moving. Angelika to breed from."

"Foolish talk," Alois muttered. He unfolded his long form, erect enough to make him seem younger than his seventy-one years, and raised his arm and his voice together to let his approval show clear. "Hail Johanna! Ho-la! Home from *Vorschaß!*"

Johanna pivoted toward the sound of her name. The morning sun set off the blond in the crown of braids above a smoothly tanned brow. Her eyes were guarded, but she smiled and lifted her cane in response.

"Livestock well off?" called the Wainwright, and again Johanna raised her cane and nodded, but her smile faded.

As they left Bengat behind them and turned onto the path that cut across the south end of the village toward Bent Elbow, Angelika moved up to speak to her sister.

"You needn't take offense," she said. "They ask the same of every man coming down from spring alp, you know they do."

Johanna tossed her head. "They can't wait for us to make a mistake."

They walked on in silence for close to an hour in the hot morning sun. Then Mikatrin began chafing against the harness that kept her in her basket; she wiggled one shoulder free and hollered, delighted. Angelika set out to loosen the straps as the cart moved along.

"We will make mistakes, you know," she muttered, struggling with the squirming child as she lifted her out of the basket. "I don't know that we can handle the haying without Hans."

"Well, I know," Johanna said shortly. "As long as the weather cooperates, we'll be fine."

"The weather don't always cooperate," Angelika persisted. "And the Lord knows what might happen with you gone every second night."

Mikatrin began to howl, bending her body at odd angles in Angelika's arms. "Down!" she demanded. "Wanna walk!"

"We'll never get home at this rate," Angelika sighed as she set the child on her feet. Mikatrin shot her mother a triumphant grin and set off after Johanna.

"You are a contrary thing," Johanna said, her voice creaky with reluctant admiration. With an apologetic smile to her sister she lifted Mikatrin, hugged her, and then set her down again. The child put her small damp hand into Johanna's.

"Tell me what will be left to hay if all the animals are grazing the home pasture," Johanna said to her sister. "Can you tell me that?"

When Angelika was silent, Johanna nodded. "It can't be done. Admit it."

"Of course we can't have all the animals at the homestead. I never claimed we could," said Angelika. "But it seems to me that every third night would be enough for you to go look out after a few yearlings."

"Two yearlings and a heifer in calf," Johanna corrected her. "Not to mention the goats. You want to explain to Hans where his animals are if one of them takes sick and nobody's there to see after it?"

Angelika put out her lip. "You know I am fearful to be at Bent Elbow alone at night."

Johanna noted to herself once again that Mikatrin came by her stubborn nature honestly. "I can't see that you have much to fear."

Angelika stepped out suddenly and placed herself square in the road, causing Johanna to draw up and stop. Beside her, Nero came to a halt, neighing softly in surprise. Angelika put the flat of her hand on her sister's shoulder and turned her to the southeast. "If you set out walking hard and didn't stop for two weeks—for ten days if you knew the way—where would you be? You'd be on the Southern Front. Just as quick that Front could be right here, couldn't it?"

"There's no other way," said Johanna, torn between an urge to shake her sister and to comfort her. "If you know of some other fix to this situation we're in, I hope you're not keeping it from me."

As abruptly as Angelika's outburst had come, it was over; her shoulders rolled inward and her face fell. "I'm only asking you not to go to the Steeple every second night."

Johanna flushed red, the color flowing up over her cheeks. Fine lines deepened around her mouth; her head tilted to one side as if its weight were suddenly too much for her neck to bear.

"Sister?"

"Looks like you won't have to worry about being alone," Johanna said, pointing with her cane.

Angelika spun around.

At the fork in the road that snaked down to Ackenau and eventually to the Rhine Valley, a man had turned toward them.

Even from a distance they could see how the infantry uniform sagged on rack-like shoulders. His left arm was in a sling.

Nero danced sideways as Angelika took off, bare heels kicking the hem of her skirt, apron fluttering, sun hat flying up and away, arms outstretched toward her husband.

"Däta," announced Mikatrin in a conversational tone, and then she put her thumb in her mouth.

"A-yo," agreed Johanna. "Your Däta's come home."

The cows wandered off into pasture that was not theirs to graze, but Johanna stood immobile in the middle of the road, her sister's child at her side. She raised her eyes toward the cliffs of the Third Sister and felt the summer's heat on her face, already on fire with disappointment and shame: disappointment for well-laid plans gone sour, shame to be wishing her brother-in-law anywhere else, even in an unmarked battlefield grave, anywhere but on this road, come home to lay claim to what was rightfully his.

Late that night, when the creaking of the bedstead in the next room woke Johanna for the second time, she rolled herself into a ball on the far edge of her mattress, buried her face in her pillow, and began to whisper her prayers out loud. She listed for herself and her God the things she had to be grateful for: animals fat on mountain grass; new cheeses well set, glowing like stacks of small, pale moons in the dimness of the cellar; Mikatrin's straight legs, her solemn face, the smell of her neck; the coming of the summer and the haying weather.

The breeze from the open window was warm, but Johanna pulled her comforter up and around her head.

She thanked God for her brother-in-law: that his injury was minor but still enough to keep him here a good six weeks, the hardest weeks of the haying season. With him at home, looking after his own concerns, Johanna could go back to Gunta Steeple.

The alp at Gunta Steeple, with its pastures and long, low structure—half barn, half living quarters—was the only thing of value left to Angelika and Johanna by their father; Angelika's half of the holdings had gone to Hans when she married him. Even so, it was the only place where Johanna felt at ease. From May to late September, when the snows drove her away, she had a home of her own. Now she would go back to sleep alone in the sparsely furnished rooms scoured clean by sharp, cold winds. She could wake at dawn in the generous silence of the Three Sisters and feel them wrapped around her like an embrace. In the day, when the work was done, while the animals grazed the endless mountain pastures, she could let Nero take her into the hidden valleys and secret places. On Nero's back a crippled leg mattered not at all.

26   Soft laughter, whispers, a gasp.

When the hay was in the barn and Hans was healed, she would have the homestead back and the farm would be hers to run. Johanna thanked God that when six weeks had passed, Hans would be going back to join his regiment on the Eastern Front.

It turned out that Hans couldn't manage a scythe with his arm in the sling, and that Johanna would have to cut the hay after all. In the late afternoon she finished the first parcel and stood to look over her work, pulling her bodice away from her skin, tacky with sweat. Hans and Angelika could rake and turn this, Johanna reckoned; in two days, she would come back from alp and Nero would haul the ricks to the hay barn while she mowed the next parcel. This plan pleased her, but there was a worry: somehow, she knew, she would have to make Hans believe he had thought of it not just alone, but against her advice. So deeply was Johanna entrenched in working out this last detail that she did not see Hans coming toward her across the field, and she jumped at the sound of his voice. The smell of the new-cut grass rose up in hot waves.

"Johanna." Hans let her name go reluctantly, like a man holding on to something he didn't put much value on but called his own anyway. He swiped at his knee with his hat. His eyes darted up cautiously to move along the line of her neck, stop at her chin, drop. He tried to smile but managed only to grimace.

She squinted at him from under the rim of her sun hat, uneasy. "I'm done here," she said.

"I have seen things," Hans responded, the words tumbling out of him in a thin stream. He was close enough for Johanna to see that he had lost a back tooth and that the shadows under his eyes were gray.

"Things to make a man think through his life," he continued. "I learned some lessons."

"That's good to know," Johanna said slowly, and she gave him a tight smile, feeling her resolve and self-control seeping away. "I expect that means you've learned the value of what you own. And what you don't." She gathered herself together, and then she looked him straight in the eye. "I'm going up to the Steeple to see to the livestock."

His jaw worked a bit, and Johanna saw something she could not at first believe: his eyes were shiny with unshed tears. This struck her as nothing else could; she let the scythe fall to the ground with a small thud.

She wiped her brow. "I wish you well, I surely do. But you can do without me."

Hans cleared his throat and sent her a sidelong glance. It was a look she knew well, one that always set her teeth on edge: he couldn't look her in the eye when he gave her an order. "We need you," he said gruffly, gesturing out over the grass still to be cut.

"I'll be back in two days to mow the next parcel," she said. "We'll get this load under cover then."

And Johanna waited for him to list the reasons she

shouldn't, couldn't go, the work she had to do, the way he wanted things done.

At that moment, the church bell began to toll in the village. Johanna startled at the tinny sound; she could not get used to this poor substitute for the old bell, requisitioned by the army for its brass. But still she raised her head, as Hans did, to count the number of times it tolled: fourteen, for the death of a man, full grown.

"Hänslar's Jok has been poorly for weeks now," Johanna said.

"It'll be a soldier," Hans said flatly.

Before she could stop herself, the words were spoken. "Could have been you," Johanna said.

Hans started toward the house, settling his hat on his head. "Could have been," he agreed.

When Johanna rode up two days later, Mikatrin came running to wind her fists in her aunt's skirts, and no amount of comforting would make her turn Johanna loose. It took sharp words from Hans before the child let go, and then she fell to sobbing: hard, wrathful tears that never eased while Johanna swung the scythe up and down the length of the field.

That evening, Angelika handed Mikatrin up to Johanna and watched her daughter settle into the saddle.

"She's all at odds," Angelika said. "The alp will do her good." And she blushed, because she was glad of this excuse to have Hans to herself and she knew that this was clear to everyone concerned, even the child.

Johanna did nothing to comfort her sister. She wanted to take Mikatrin; she loved the child, who would be just the right amount of company at alp. But she also knew that sooner or later, when the first flush of having Hans back in her bed had worn off, Angelika would reclaim her daughter.

* * *

When Hans had been home about five weeks, Johanna rose at dawn and saw the storm clouds gathering over the far ridges of the mountains to the south. She got Mikatrin out of bed, all warm and sweet, and bundled her up, setting off as soon as she was sure that the animals were all within range of cover. Nero didn't need to be rushed; he knew better than she did what was coming, and he moved smartly. Johanna wrapped her cape around Mikatrin and let Nero canter once they cleared Bengat.

The storm beat them, breaking over their heads in a furious downpour that made Mikatrin crow in surprise and delight. The first thunder came sudden as Johanna passed the child down to her mother in the doorway of the barn.

"Won't be anything to mow for three days at least," Angelika said.

Johanna wiped her face with the back of her hand. "Hans in the village?"

"A-yo. I expect he'll wait out the worst of the storm at the Eagle."

Nero pushed his muzzle against Johanna's shoulder, and she rubbed her knuckles along his neck.

"You won't need me here with this weather. I'll just dry out and then I'll head back."

Angelika cleared her throat. "You been working hard."

Johanna pulled the saddle from Nero's back and nodded.

"Hans appreciates everything you have done," Angelika added. "I am sorry to have to say this for him, sister." She took the bridle from Johanna and hung it up. "He also said that you were right. About not sending the animals on to high alp–"

From the open barn door they watched the trees twisting in the wind; waves of rain swelled and then receded.

Angelika turned back to Johanna, head held high, chin trembling. "I would like to keep her with us this trip," she said, hovering between apology and accusation.

The timbers popped and creaked around them. Rain

crawled over the roof. Lightning reached sharp fingers into the shadows; the thunder stepped right in. The cows shifted uneasily in the cowshed. Once again Nero pushed his muzzle into the curve of Johanna's neck. She let him rock her backwards.

"She's your daughter," Johanna said. She began to rub Nero down.

Angelika smiled in spite of herself. "Sometimes it seems she holds you dearer than she does me."

Johanna laughed, all harshness and trouble. "She has my undivided attention, that's all."

"I'm sorry if I've been caught up. It's just that he'll be going back soon..." Angelika's voice trailed off.

At the sight of his feed bag, Nero whinnied softly. Johanna took her time adjusting it for him.

"You got nothing to apologize for," she said finally. "It's not your fault that I need your roof over my head."

Angelika opened her mouth to protest, and then, with a hurt look, she shut it again.

"You'll need provisions and a change of clothes," she said.

When Johanna came upon the soldier later that day at Gunta Steeple, her first clear thought was a single word of thanks that she had left Mikatrin behind.

Wet through and through, with her cane hooked over her wrist and her arms full of firewood, Johanna had elbowed open the door between the house and the stable to find him asleep on the old settee. He was rolled onto his side with his hands under his head, his face turned away. Muddy boots hung over the edge. One lace trailed in a growing pool of water.

Johanna's second clear thought was that he was considerate; a man as weary as this one who still remembered to keep his boots clear of the upholstery must have been raised right.

This picture was still forming itself in her head—a young boy, a mother with an uplifted finger, a strange doorway in an unfamiliar place where dirty boots were left standing outside on a mat next to a pot of geraniums—when he catapulted up with a sudden twist and jerk.

They stood opposite each other across the room, Johanna with the wood in her arms, blinking hard to clear the rain from her eyelashes.

"Where's your little girl?" he asked.

She took in many things all at once: that he spoke a broad Tirolean dialect; that some of his clothes might once have been part of a uniform but were now faded and worn; that he had tried to cut the shock of dark hair that hung down over his eyes; that he was at least a few years older than she was; and that a gun leaned against the wall within his immediate reach.

And she realized that she was covered with a thin, keen sweat.

Johanna inhaled and turned away. The firewood tumbled out of her arms as if it had somehow caught her panic; her cane went with it. She staggered through the mess and over the doorsill.

"I thought you'd be gone until tomorrow," he said, coming forward.

Poised at the step, Johanna turned to face him, a hand pressed to her mouth.

He retrieved Johanna's cane and held it out to her, leaning to one side so as not to strike his head on the door frame.

"I haven't heard a human voice in two months," he said.

After a moment, when her breath came easier, Johanna answered, "You can't stay here." Then she reached forward and took her cane from him.

He crouched down to pick up the firewood, his back straight, balanced gracefully on the balls of his feet. When he looked up at her she drew back further into the storm, startled. She had not expected him to smile. She had not expected his face to open up this way, or the deep laugh lines around his eyes, or the flash of his teeth against dark skin. She had not thought that he could disarm her of her fear so easily.

"Will you let me get dry before I go?" he asked. "You are wet too. I can start a fire. I would be very glad of it myself."

"Who are you?"

He inclined his head. "Donati, Francesco."

She blinked. "Are you an Italian, or a deserter?"

"Which would frighten you more?"

"I don't know," Johanna said, distracted. "You don't talk like an Italian."

"Then I must be a deserter."

She calculated how long it would take him to catch up with her if she should turn and run for Nero.

"I won't chase you if you want to go," he said softly. "But I wish you'd stay and talk to me first."

Johanna leaned against the door frame with her wet cape wrapped around her.

"Where's your little girl?" he asked again a few minutes later. He had lit the oil lamp and was laying the fire.

"I left her at home with...my sister."

"Is your husband on the line? France?"

She looked down at her shoes and the water pooling around her. "Mostly they send our men to the South Tirol. Or east, to Galicia."

"I hope he is in Galicia, for his sake." And then, less quickly, "For your sake."

Johanna wondered at the strangeness of this, that she should feel curiosity when she thought she must feel fear. She closed her eyes and waited for it to come back and claim her, but there was only the familiar darkness.

He clearly wanted to talk. "I have a daughter, she's at home with my youngest sister."

"Where does your sister live?"

He glanced up at her. "Verona."

The calm that had started to grow between them was suddenly gone.

"You said you weren't Italian."

"No. You said I didn't talk like an Italian."

Johanna swallowed hard. "You don't. You talk like a Tirolean, but smarter."

He laughed at this, a deep, abrupt laugh. "I spent a lot of time in the Alto Adige with my mother's people. Do you know the South Tirol?"

"I have never been out of this mountain valley," Johanna said.

"My grandfather was the forest overseer for a good part of the Antholzertal. He was a tough old man."

"Then you are Austrian."

"Half, yes. Half, no. My other grandfather was a doctor, in Verona. Just as tough." He smiled, and then a sadness came over his face.

Johanna focused her gaze on the tips of her shoes. "Which half are you fighting for?" she asked without looking up.

"Neither," he said finally. "I deserted in March."

"You can't go back?" Johanna asked, against her better judgment, still not looking at him.

"When I go back, I will be shot," Francesco said. "Which is why I sit here with you."

"What about your little girl?"

"I suppose that I will never see her again," he said.

Johanna finally hung her cape by the stove and busied herself putting food on the table: cheese, bread, eggs.

"I would have taken these things without your permission if you hadn't returned," he said. "I have no way to pay you."

"I can't eat in front of a hungry man."

"Then I thank you for your generosity. And your company."

"You can sleep in that chair where you sit," Johanna said, flustered. "Or on the settee." She glanced toward the closed door to the small bedroom and wondered if he had been there. "In the morning you have to go. I won't–I won't tell anyone."

He raised an eyebrow. "I have told you that I would have stolen from you. You know only bad things about me." He paused. "Why do you trust me?"

"I can't send you out into that rain. You might wander over the cliff," Johanna said. She turned away, because she knew that this was only a half-truth, and because she feared that the rest of the truth sat plain on her face for him to see, and in the tremble of her hand as she picked up her bread. "It would take a cowardly man to hurt a woman without any means of protecting herself, in her own home," she finished.

Then Johanna raised her head and looked hard at him. She saw the creases on his knuckles, the dark hair that reached out from under the frayed cuffs, the way his sleeves strained against his upper arms. His hair was graying high on the temples; his forehead was damp with sweat. At last she let herself meet his gaze, and she saw nothing there but a little wariness.

"I have been in the mountains for three months now," he said evenly. "It has been much longer than that since I have been alone with a woman."

Johanna's bread crumbled in her hands.

He said, "I want nothing from you but your company. You don't even have to tell me your name if you don't want to."

She stared at him in surprise and undisguised pain, the muscles in her throat working silently. Before he could say a word, she took her cape from the wall and was gone.

He thought of leaving. Of heading deeper into these strange mountains, so unlike the Southern Alps and Dolomites of his boyhood, so much more gentle. It would be the safe thing to do. He had learned to think of his safety first and his stomach second. He had rationed all other thoughts strictly.

But the woman had blushed.

Francesco had feared to ask too much of her, and saw, too late, that he had asked too little. Still, his insensitivity had brought a return: it had sparked an incredible bloom of color, and he had seen what she must have looked like as a young girl.

At night, when he dared to list for himself the things he would never see again, Francesco had sometimes thought of blushes like the one she had given him: it had seeped over her face and risen even to the pale skin at the first blond hairs high on her forehead. He thought of that same color spreading over the white skin of her neck. He thought of it on her shoulders and at the first swelling of her breasts.

Francesco watched the fire and thought of the woman. One part of him, the small kernel inside him that was still a boy, wanted to go after her, to find her sitting in the hay among the animals, her arms wrapped around her knees. He stayed where he was because he knew that this would frighten her, and he did not want to see the fright in her eyes. It would be better never to see her again.

The soldier knew how to wait. He could not change what would happen: she would come, or she would not.

When she looked in the window, hours later, Francesco had fallen asleep at the table with his head on his arms. His rifle leaned against the wall just behind him, and the barrel of a pistol lay against his thigh, gleaming weakly in the light of the lamp.

Hans and Angelika looked up in surprise from the breakfast skillet when Johanna came in. Mikatrin, her face smeared with mush, waved a spoon.

"Hanna!" she yelled.

Johanna leaned over the table and kissed the child's sticky cheek.

"You must have set out before sunrise," said Hans.

"Yes, I did. I forgot some things."

"Do you have a fever?" Angelika asked, coming to lay a hand on her sister's brow. "Are you sick? You look tired."

Johanna brushed her hand away. "I'm fine," she said irritably. "Didn't sleep well." Then, quickly, she hugged her sister.

Surprised, Angelika patted Johanna's back. "What's got into you?"

"Nothing," Johanna answered. "Not a thing."

"Livestock well off?" asked Hans.

"Right as rain," said Johanna, and turned away to fetch a cup from the shelf.

"Stay until tomorrow," Angelika said. "I was going to bake. You can take some cake with you."

"At least you can stay long enough to help with the cheese," Hans said.

Johanna found her spoon in the table drawer and leaned in over the skillet, which sat on its trivet in the middle of the table. She busied herself with the *Stopfar*, spooning the fried farina into her milk cup, watching the golden butterfat rise from the crisp mass. When she had eaten three spoonfuls soaked in milk, she looked up at her sister.

"I have to go back," she said. "I want to."

"You'd think you had a treasure hidden up there," Angelika chided her gently, "instead of some raggedy half-wild stock."

"She's half wild herself," Hans pointed out.

Angelika clucked at him.

"He's right," Johanna told her sister, bending over her cup again. "Don't scold the man for telling the truth."

Johanna worked until after dinner. In the early afternoon she set out, not on the direct route through the village, but up through the forests of beech and oak, hawthorn and ash, that covered the lower slopes of the Praying Hands. Nero picked his way delicately over vague trails, steep and slick, his sides clenching. They found their way out of the first tree line and headed up toward the ridges where the heart of the storm had settled, pulling in layers of cloud like shawls over bony shoulders.

Once Johanna paused to look down toward the village and saw that it had disappeared. She was alone in a world grown suddenly unfamiliar and indistinct around her, the warm rain soaking through the boiled wool of her cape and hood.

Nero climbed over the last crest in the late afternoon. Johanna felt as though he were delivering her directly into heaven: the rocky knolls and cliff walls that framed the fan-shaped pasture were suspended in cloud, wrapped in layers of loosely spun haze. In some places the mist was impenetrable, a wall of reflected light, pearly whites and grays. Then it would shift lazily and open itself to reveal some small treasure: the spire of rock that gave the Steeple its name; a patch of gullies and ravines twisting like gnarled fingers; the cowshed, weathered shingles glistening with wet.

The mist closed in, and Johanna watched the building disappear. She waited, motionless, until it drifted back into view. A small stand of blue spruce. The stable door. The outhouse. The watering trough and pump. A rush of sunlight, unexpected and painfully bright, cavorted wildly on the tin chimneypiece. Then it was all gone again.

Nero felt his way forward. Sounds were muffled in the mist, echoing unevenly; the animals first seemed to be grazing far away in the meadow, then to have vanished, then to be directly before Nero. Johanna pulled him up, expecting him to collide with a surprised yearling. When he came to a halt at the stable door, she saw that the animals had all sought shelter. They looked up at her blankly and were not distracted from their cud, even when she went about the tasks they depended upon.

Johanna hesitated at the door that led into the living quarters. She imagined the empty rooms, the bread crumbs on the table, the cold stove. So clearly did she see these things in her mind's eye that when she opened the door to Francesco, sitting in the dim room in the same chair where she had left him, she thought he might be another trick of the storm, just mist and light and strange, half-realized wishes.

"I asked you to go," she said hoarsely.

"I lied," Francesco said, rising from his chair.

Johanna froze.

"I want more than just your company. I want to know everything about you. But I was afraid to frighten you away, and I was clumsy. Forgive me."

She said, "I have no husband, no children. I work to earn my keep on my brother-in-law's homestead. This place–it's all I have."

"You have a name. Please tell me your name."

"Johanna," she said, blushing furiously. "My name is Johanna."

"What do you do for a living?" she asked him after a supper of goat's milk and bread spread thick with new butter.

He reached into the battered knapsack under the table and drew out a sheaf of papers, which he unfolded before her, spreading his hands over the creases.

"I'm a cartographer. This has been my diary since I left the Front."

Johanna bent her head over the maps. A strand of her hair, white blond in the lamplight, fell across the paper.

He reached out toward it with one finger; his touch ran like light up the length of a single hair, through her scalp, down her spine.

She tucked the hair into the braids that circled her head.

"You blush like a schoolgirl," he said softly.

"I am thirty-seven years old." Johanna smiled. "Hardly a girl."

"I wonder."

"Explain your maps to me," she said, her voice shaky.

"These are contour lines. Cliffs, ridges, saddles. Animal tracks, logging trails, forest. You see, a different symbol for each sort of tree—beech, copper beech, white pine, spruce, oak, ash, maple, yew—"

He pulled his chair closer to hers, and she could feel how eager he was, how much he wanted to show her these sheets covered with the evidence of his industry and skill.

"I began here." His finger hovered over peaks drawn in clean, sparse pencil strokes. Each bore a tiny name, carefully lettered: *Croda Rossa, Cristallo, P. Tre Croci, Col. S. Angelo.* "The scale here is relatively good. I had the field maps to work from."

He considered for a moment.

"There was still a lot of snow. There were small avalanches—here and here. Sometimes I was forced to go much deeper into the valleys. Into the villages, at night, or I would have frozen. Or starved."

"Were they looking for you?" Johanna asked.

He shrugged.

"How did you eat?"

"I stole. Once I stood in the dark and swallowed a whole strudel. It was still steaming. I had blisters in my mouth for days. Another time I chopped wood for an old blind woman. She called me Markus, she thought I was her son. She gave me fresh bread and let me drink my fill of milk."

His face went slack with remembering. "Milk was the thing I missed the most. Once I stole a goat just to milk her."

"Milk is the only thing we have a lot of," Johanna said.

"In the trenches we sometimes had condensed milk. It

tasted of the tin it came in." Francesco rubbed his forehead. "Here, at the Engadine border, my field maps ended and I had to work from memory, with very basic tools. So what you see here is the Austria of my own mind and eyes." His finger moved up a map. "I kept west, then north."

"Why didn't you stay in Engadine?"

"The Swiss would have just sent me back."

"They do that? They send soldiers back?"

Francesco let his eyes wander over her face. "You are very protected from the war here," he said.

"We get news weeks late, unless someone is killed—" She paused. "Don't you want to know how the war is going?"

"No," he said quickly, and he smiled with such grim intensity that Johanna shifted on her chair. She cleared her throat; Francesco ran a hand through his hair and took up his story again.

"After the Silvretta I didn't know the names of the peaks anymore, so I named them myself, after my sisters. Verena, Ariane, Maria, Elena. This is where I was when the first real warm weather broke. I named the peak Marta, after my youngest sister. There's a high alp on the ridge just below—"

"Shadona. My grandfather once had a share of that alp, some years ago."

"I was there until the alpler drove the cows in." He smiled at her. "And now I'm here. You don't send your animals to high alp?"

"We couldn't afford a share," Johanna said.

"That is my good fortune."

Johanna leaned back over the map. "Is Marta the sister who looks after your daughter?"

"Yes. She took Olivia in when I was called up."

"Your wife?"

"She died five years ago. When Olivia was eight."

"I'm sorry."

He nodded.

"What did you do when you ran out of sisters?"

"I named the mountains after women in the literature I remembered from school: Griselda, Héloïse, Beatrice, Desdemona, Iphigenia."

She touched a finger lightly to the map. "Orietta? Laura? Angela? Are these from stories?"

His eyes, deep brown, were edged with green. He hesitated, and then he shook his head.

"Laura was the name of a woman–Petrarch wrote poems about her. But Laura was also my wife's name. Those are the names of women I have loved."

Johanna sat back in her chair and folded her hands in her lap. She wanted to get up and go away, because if she didn't she might bend her head back down to the map under the circle of light. She was afraid that in the carefully drawn, precisely detailed world he had created for himself out of his past and present, she would see that there was not room enough for another name. All of this passed over her face; she felt it, and she could see Francesco taking it in. That made it all much more excruciating, and at the same time, easier, because he was looking at her evenly, without a hint of pity or disdain.

"Now I know you are Italian," she said, trying to smile but failing. "No Austrian would ever think of that. Or if he did, he wouldn't admit it."

"Every soldier thinks such things. Especially on the Front."

He was very close. She smelled him: the faint sweetness of tobacco long gone, the sharpness of yellow soap, the taint of sweat ground deep into rough fabric and boot leather.

Johanna said, "I have to look after the animals."

This time he knew she would come back. He had seen it in the set of her jaw, and in the resolute line of her back as she went through the little door into the stable.

Francesco thought once again of leaving. He was enraptured, deeply aroused, terribly frightened. He imagined her hair spread out over a pillow, a silky golden web; he imagined the satiny, cradle-like underside of her. She would rock him into oblivion and he would go there gladly, and once he had gone that far, once he had forgotten how to run and survive, he would remember why he had wanted to live.

He looked at his hands, hard and calloused, and he wondered how he would ever find the kindness she would expect of him, the tender words, the gentleness she deserved. Things he had known once but had left behind him in the trenches, their weight too much to carry through strange mountains.

When she returned the room was lit only by a glimpse of the fire through the stove grating. She hung her cape on the wall next to his greatcoat, and when she was able, she turned to face him. Moving across the floor, she was afraid of losing her balance even with her cane.

He sat in the corner of the broad settee. He had taken off his gunbelt, but his shirt was still buttoned to the neck, a courtesy that touched her and frightened her all at once. Johanna stood before him, the fingers of her right hand wound in her skirt.

"The storm is worse," she said softly.

Francesco's face was a complex of shadows, solemn and yet relaxed. He put a hand on her hip, gently, tentatively. His warmth radiated through layers of material to embrace the thickened, foreshortened bone; she covered his hand with her own. He drew her down next to him, and for a while they sat listening to the muted clank of bells as the animals settled in for the night, the hissing of the fire, the rain and wind rising in whispers around them.

Johanna's heart kept beating when she thought it must stop. She knew that it was still beating, because she could feel it at her temples and in the soft flesh on the inside of her elbows and in her belly. There is still time to end this, she told herself, but she knew that was not true: she could not. She did not want to walk away.

"If I were a younger man, I would tell you how your hair reminds me of the gold and white of new down. I would call you *Paparella*. Duckling."

Johanna inhaled. "If I were younger, I would think you were making fun of my limp."

Francesco's hand tightened on her wrist. "Then I will call you *Fragolina* instead. Little Strawberry. For your blushes."

She shook her head weakly, and dropped her chin.

Then he said, "Tell me what you want above all things in the world."

Surprised, Johanna smiled. "I want to live here all year. If the snow didn't chase me away, I would do it. I would manage, somehow."

"That's all?" he asked, moved by the simplicity and the impossibility of her wish.

Her forehead furrowed and her mouth set hard. At first he thought she was angry, but then he saw how things were with her, all the untapped compassion and tenderness exposed; he bent forward to put his brow against her temple.

"Listen to me."

She waited.

"Johanna. I am as frightened as you are."

Three days later, when the weather had broken and Johanna knew the grass would be dry enough to cut, she rode down the mountain. She sat straight in the saddle, aware as she had never been before of the rhythmic rocking and the way the worn leather chafed, aware that there was a new smell about her now, in her clothes and hair, rising from her skin.

Angelika had been watching, and she set off to meet her sister on the little incline to the house. She stood there with her hand pressed to her chest, her face shiny and tight, as Johanna approached.

"He's gone," she said before Johanna could dismount.

"Hans?"

"They said he was well enough to go back. He left yesterday. He was going to come up and talk to you before–"

Johanna drew in a sharp breath at this, but Angelika went on, unseeing. "But there wasn't time, in the end." Her face worked and twisted as if to ban the tears that blinded her.

"I'll get on with the haying," Johanna said finally, strangely deflated.

"You'll stay tonight?" Angelika asked, clutching at Johanna's skirt.

Caught in the maelstrom of her own anger and sorrow, Angelika did not see these very same things on her sister's face. She did not see that Johanna was flushed with a new empathy; she did not notice that her sister looked at her with different eyes.

"Yes," Johanna said. "I'll stay tonight. But tomorrow I'll have to go, once the hay is in."

Angelika wiped her face with the corner of her apron. "It's the nights that are so hard," she said. "As long as you stay the nights."

The next afternoon, Angelika came to watch her sister pack. She spoke up with a little rush of breath.

"Tell me why you turned the Wainwright down last year when he made you an offer."

Johanna looked at her, surprised. "Why are you bringing that up again?"

"I want to know."

"Why should I have accepted him? He didn't want me, he was just desperate."

"You would have had a home of your own." Then, realizing how this must sound, Angelika put a hand to her mouth.

But Johanna only laughed. "And a shop to run. I'd rather be a servant," she said, but a hard look came over her face.

Angelika lifted her chin. "That's unfair."

"Maybe."

"Maybe you should have accepted him," Angelika shot back, her hurt and anger pushing her on. "At least you might have had a child of your own. Maybe a child would have been worth giving up the Steeple for."

Johanna was silent, but her face flooded with deep color.

Angelika was dismayed at the depths of the cruelty she had found within herself. Still, when the next thought came to her, she was unable to do anything but offer it.

She said, "You did the right thing."

"How do you mean?"

"You can't miss what you've never had. You can't lose something you don't own." And she spread out her hands before her as if to pass on a lesson worth learning.

Johanna's face convulsed with scorn.

"You haven't lost anything yet," she said. "You don't know the meaning of the word."

Johanna found Francesco in the *Stadel* perched on the edge of the milking stool, the nanny goat caught between his knees. The kid stood off to the side, bleating indignantly. Johanna shooed it back out to pasture, and then she leaned against the open doorway, arms crossed, head to one side, to watch. She forced her breathing to quiet, she willed her heart to stop galloping.

"My grandmother had goats," Francesco said over his

shoulder. "I could never get enough of her goat cheese." He rose.

When he was close enough for her to feel his breath on her skin, Francesco held the edge of the bucket to her lips and she drank. She coughed a little; milk ran down from the corner of her mouth. With the palm of his hand, he wiped it away.

"You've been a long time," he said, putting the bucket down. "I was worried. I thought about coming to look for you."

"You would have had to ask the way."

Francesco inclined his head, a little dip left as one brow arched. "I usually find what I'm looking for. Maybe I have already come looking."

"You wouldn't. You might be seen," she said.

"I could say that I am your distant cousin from the Antholzertal."

Johanna snorted. "The women in the village know my family tree better than I do."

"A distant lover, then." And laughing out loud at the blush this called forth, he leaned in closer. "Why have you put your hair back up?"

She touched a finger to the braids pinned around her head. "Because I would draw attention to myself if I didn't."

"Now, that is true," he said, pulling pins out and letting them drop to the ground. "But what a shame to hide this hair."

His fingers tangled in her braids as they fell to her shoulders; she caught a hand and pulled it behind her to hold at the small of her back.

"My brother-in-law has gone back to the line," she said.

Francesco paused and something flitted across his face: fear, thought Johanna, and then, correcting herself: pity.

"I can't stay long," she told him.

"Until the morning?"

She dropped her head, her lips pressed tight together.

"Until morning?" he asked again, tilting up her chin.

"I can't stay the night."

"I'm afraid to be alone," he said playfully.

Johanna laughed. "You're teasing me. But that's just what my sister said, and she meant it."

"But I mean what I say, too, Johanna. Think, if you go back down to your sister tonight, three of us sleep alone. If you stay here with me, then only she sleeps alone."

"I mustn't be selfish," she whispered, even as she let him coax her into the depths of a kiss so soft that she knew she was in danger of drowning. He held her so close that she wondered, with some part of her mind that was always striving to be separate, to observe, that a human body could be so solid, every muscle so slate-hard that veins surfaced to pulse just under the skin, endless rivers to be navigated by fingertip. His strength, the energy and force that lay abeyant in his arms–the fact that she could have him right now, or stop him: these were things to make her drunk and foolish with contentment.

"Stay," he murmured, his mouth poised above hers, his hands sliding under her blouse so that her skin rose and shimmered to his touch. Strong fingers claimed a bare shoulder, the thumb resting at the hollow of her throat.

"Until morning," Johanna agreed. Caught once more in the trance of his kiss, she was surprised, in a distracted way, at how easy it was to do this. How easy it was to put aside all thought of her sister, sleeping alone while youth ran out of her. How easy it was to be selfish, for once.

At dawn he was reluctant to let her go; when she tried to open the door, he leaned over her to hold it shut, one hand braced against the frame.

"When will you come back?"

Johanna pivoted to face him, arching her back against the door.

"As soon as I can. Will you wait?"

"As long as I can," he said.

Her face tightened and shifted at this, the first word that had fallen between them about what would eventually come to pass.

She ducked away and moved to the other side of the room. There she looked over the things he had spread out on the table: compass and calipers and pencils, stubs of candle, his pocketknife and whetstone, a shaving brush and soap and a straight razor. A map was centered under the hanging lamp; she bent her head to look at it.

Suddenly she turned to him, her face ashen.

"You've gone further up the valley. The north face of the Praying Hands–you can't see that from here. Or Grenat's Horn or Little Calf Lake."

He took the paper from her and let it fall to the floor. "I've had a look," he said.

Johanna stood with her arms at her sides and stared at the square of paper.

"I should have thought to bring you maps."

Francesco considered his answer. "Yes," he said finally. "Maps would be a help to me."

Her face contorted with worry. "You don't feel safe here."

"Ask me instead if I am happy here with you."

Johanna trembled a little when he put his arms around her.

With his forehead pressed against her temple, he said, "I am happy here with you."

She tried to pull away from him, but he would not let her go.

"Johanna," he whispered. "I'm not going anywhere for a good while." And then, his voice hoarser, "I haven't had enough of your blushes." He was glad she could not see his face; for once he was unable to smile.

"Promise me something."

"I'll try."

"Go while I'm away. Don't tell me ahead of time. Can you promise me that?"

After a long while, Francesco nodded.

When Johanna was home, Angelika went about her work in silence. In the weeks since Hans left she had given up trying to convince her sister to spend more nights at the homestead, but she muttered under her breath while Johanna packed provisions and kissed Mikatrin goodbye. Johanna bore all this with an evenness of temper that seemed to drive Angelika further from her.

Sometimes, on her way down the mountain and away from Francesco, Johanna was able to think of other things, of her real life, and to wonder if she would ever be able to heal the rift between herself and her sister. She thought of telling Angelika the truth; she tried to imagine a sister who would not begrudge her these few weeks of something Angelika herself knew and treasured. But Johanna was unable to picture anything but accusation and distaste in her sister's eyes.

Then, eight weeks after the storm that had brought Francesco to her, Johanna realized that the day was coming when she would have to confess. When the first snows forced her away from the Steeple, when he was gone, the evidence of the time she had spent with him would show itself. At first this thought filled Johanna with terror, and then, slowly, with joy and a reckless pride.

Johanna was asleep in the early afternoon, curled like an infant in Francesco's arms on a bed hatched with squares of sunlight, when someone came up over the last crest, calling her name.

Francesco woke instantly, and was out of the bed and

moving around the room before Johanna understood fully what she had heard.

He retrieved his gun and boots and with one hand pulled her to her feet, smoothed the cloud of hair that trailed around her, and pushed her out of the bedroom toward the door.

It was the tension in the set of his jaw, returned so absolutely and so suddenly, that shook her awake. Johanna breathed in Francesco's fear, and her mouth filled with an acrid saliva that she could not swallow.

She thought of the high pasture where they had spent the morning. She remembered him standing in the frigid water of a stream, trouser legs rolled up around his calves. She remembered the way he had laughed when she turned her mouth down and refused to join him. She thought of his hands on her upper arms, and how it felt to be lifted up and set on bare feet in water so cold that every shade of blue and green the mountains had to offer began to glow.

Johanna remembered all these things, and she was overwhelmed by anger, that someone should intrude here and change everything simply by calling her name. With her blood rushing in her ears so that she could barely hear, she went to the door and opened it.

Bengat's Alois came toward her, waving his hat in greeting; before she could step out to meet him he was under the lip of the roof.

She dare not close the door; it was an act too rude to go unnoticed.

Francesco stood in the shadows, his back pressed to the wall. Johanna thought she could hear him breathing.

"Day, Johanna," Alois greeted her, his smile dying on his face.

Alois did not know what to make of the sight of a grown woman with her hair flying free and disheveled around her in the middle of the day. Worse, her blouse was open at the neck, she wore no apron, and the thin pleats of her *Juppa* were crushed beyond smoothing. And her color. Her color made Alois think of his Isabella, when she had come to his bed for the first time on their wedding night. This picture, unbidden, startled him with its tender power.

Johanna nodded at him, struggling to gather her wits. "Day, Alois." She looked over his shoulder. "A surprise to see you up here."

He raised an eyebrow at her tone, and Johanna drew up a little, ashamed of herself.

"Nice to have the company," she murmured.

"A-yo," he said, rubbing a splayed thumb across the bridge of his nose. "Haven't been up this way in a while." He took measure of the Three Sisters crowding in on the narrow meadow and the animals grazing there.

"Yearlings looking perky. You thinking of putting them on the market soon?"

Johanna smiled. "It's that or the butcher," she said, falling into the easy rhythm of this ancient conversation, knowing what was expected of her. "Couldn't keep them in hay over the winter. You interested?"

"Might be," he drawled. "Why don't you invite an old man in and offer him a drink, see what kind of bargain you can drive." He peered up at her with a half-grin, his head cocked to one side. "Or maybe you got somebody hid in there?"

Suddenly, Johanna was as clear and cold as the stream where she had waded with Francesco this morning. Her thoughts ran just as sure and fast away and down the Second Sister, and then south. They swept over the Dolomites, where he had fought and where he had chosen to stop fighting, yellow and white limestone walls and towers and buttresses against the southern blue sky, flecked with blood and flesh, echoing with artillery fire and the shouts of the dying. Her thoughts ran with the waters of the Adige and on to Verona. They stopped there, at a small house where a young girl sat on a terrace of red stone in the late August sunlight, wondering where her father was, if he was really dead as her aunts seemed to think, or if he would come home some day.

Alois's grin faded. His eyes flickered: once, twice, and without turning Johanna knew that Francesco stood in the open door behind her.

She put out her chin, her mouth grim and pale. "Let me make you acquainted," Johanna said. "My cousin from the Antholzertal. Franz."

"I prefer Francesco," he murmured as he stepped forward to offer his hand.

Alois was looking between them; he seemed to be reckoning something out for himself. Then he straightened his shoulders and nodded. He shook Francesco's hand.

"I suppose you must be kin to Senno Stante's Dokus, who settled down that way some many years ago. Handled cheese." But this was not a question, and he turned away before Francesco was obliged to answer or respond in any way.

"I'd be glad to sit here with you and your cousin for a while." He settled down on the step and cleared his throat.

"I nearly forgot why I came all the way up here. I am a forgetful old man, you know. My Bella is always commenting on it."

Alois paused to look up the valley.

"We had a summer like this, sweet grass and hot weather, when the Seven Weeks' War came along. I remember turning hay and cursing my brother Bartle because the homestead couldn't spare me but he got to go off and fight the Prussians. Did you know they billeted the whole regiment in Ackenau before they moved them out to Königsgrätz?"

Johanna shook her head, because she could not speak. Alois didn't seem to notice.

"And Bartle marched down the road along with Kolobano

Kaspar's Kaspar and Hickar's Tonile, and they were laughing as they went, and the sun was shining so bright you could count the needles on the trees, and I thought it was the end of the world that I couldn't go fight with them. Twenty-one years old, and I thought my life was over."

He turned and looked up at Francesco. "I was that much of a boy back in '66."

Francesco's face shifted and a muscle in his cheek fluttered. His eyes were over-bright, and Johanna thought for one frightening moment that he was going to cry. Instead he smiled, an awkward, thankful smile, and she understood that something had passed between the old man and Francesco that she had missed, was meant to miss, and was not to ask about.

Alois cleared his throat again. "Johanna, I am sorry to keep getting away from the point of my visit. I'm here to fetch you home."

He held up his hand as if she had tried to interrupt him.

"It's Angelika. Just a woman problem of some kind, nothing to call the priest about. But she can't manage the milking, and I can't get all the way out to Bent Elbow twice a day to lend a hand."

The heat of the afternoon was suddenly heavy on Johanna, and she rocked on her heels, leaning back against Francesco. Then, with tremendous effort, she willed herself to focus.

"That's kind of you, and I thank you for your trouble."

"I wish I could be more help. You had an uncommon lot of work on your shoulders this season. Done real well, too. Your daddy would have been proud of you—"

Surprised, Johanna began to stutter in reply, but he went on.

"No, it's true. A good farmer deserves a word of praise now and then," he said.

Then he fell silent, to leave her to herself for a moment with those words he had given her: *a good farmer.*

Later, when Alois had gone on his way, Francesco took

his place on the step and sat quietly, looking out over the little valley. Johanna stood beside him, and he wrapped his arm around her legs and laid his head against her thigh.

After a while he pulled her down to sit beside him on the step. Then, with fingers grown suddenly slow and clumsy, he smoothed and braided her hair.

Angelika and Mikatrin were huddled together in bed, Mikatrin's teary face bedded on her father's pillow. The child leapt up at the sight of her aunt and flung herself into Johanna's arms.

"I'm glad you're here," Angelika said evenly, as if Johanna had come to tea on a Sunday afternoon.

"What is it?" Johanna's voice crackled. Mikatrin hiccuped against her shoulder, and she soothed her as best she could.

"I started bleeding last night," Angelika said. "I got over to Bengat to ask for help this morning, but then I couldn't get back for dizziness."

Johanna sat down heavily on the edge of the bed, and Mikatrin climbed off her lap into the space between her mother and her aunt.

"Do you need help? A doctor?"

Angelika grimaced a little, but shook her head. "The worst of it seems to be over." And then she smiled up at Johanna, a weak half-smile that struck to the heart. "Good thing I didn't tell Hans about this baby yet."

In the silence that fell between them, Johanna turned her attention to the window opposite the bed. Storm clouds were gathering in the north in great fists of yellow and gray and terrible, bruised plum; she watched them churning, trailing ragged veils of rain behind them. The storm was moving away from Bent Elbow, and this was more than Johanna could bear: tears pressed hot behind her eyes and then they came, in a silent, ferocious rush.

Angelika put a cold hand on her wrist. "Please don't take on so," she said.

Johanna jerked away from her. "As soon as you're up to being on your own for a day, I'll drive the livestock home."

"I thought we'd all move back for the fall–," Angelika began.

"No."

Confused and suddenly very worried, Angelika regarded her sister. "But we have to. The hay won't last otherwise. You know that."

"No," Johanna repeated, her throat tight with tears.

"Listen," Angelika said after a long silence. "I know you're worried about me, but I'll be fine. We can move back to the Steeple. I'm looking forward to it. Just the three of us, it'll be like it was in the spring."

Johanna's face crumpled. She covered her eyes with her hands.

"My God," Angelika whispered. And then, "Please."

A small whimpering came from Mikatrin, a lonely and frightened sound; Johanna raised her head and looked at the child in surprise. She put her arms out and Mikatrin collapsed into her embrace.

"You see," Angelika said, her voice wavering. "You see how much we need you. We'll be together at the Steeple for the fall season, and it will be like none of this ever happened."

Johanna nodded and turned away, her mouth filling with the bitter taste of Angelika's love and gratitude.

That night Mikatrin was unsettled and wakeful.

"It's all the trouble," Angelika said, leaning against the door as she watched Johanna try to calm the child. "She's bound to feel it."

Johanna brushed the damp hair away from Mikatrin's face.

"Maybe a walk," Angelika said, rubbing the dark half-moons under her own eyes. "Maybe some night air would do her good."

Johanna carried the child out of the house and started up the stone path in the darkness. Mikatrin folded her arms around Johanna's neck and hummed a little with the rising of a breeze; Johanna tucked the blanket closer in around her and leaned more heavily on her cane.

In the moonlight the pastures climbed silver and gray toward the forest, where endless armies of trees stood silent watch in the darkness. Above them the mountains stretched into the night sky. Johanna could feel the autumn hovering there, in the skeletal fingers of the Praying Hands, on the winding ridges where the Three Sisters bent their heads to whisper together. The first snow was not far off; it would lay claim to everything green and growing, creeping down from the highest places to possess the alp as well, tenacious and miserly, a jealous lover.

On a boulder at the side of the path, Johanna sat down to rest, and Mikatrin curled gratefully into her lap.

In the woods on the cliff just above the homestead there was a rustling. Johanna froze.

Mikatrin lifted her head and blinked into the darkness.

"What do you hear?" Johanna asked, breathless. "What do you see?"

Without answering, the child let the weight of her head pull her back to the warmth and comfort of Johanna's breast, and she gave herself over to sleep.

Isabella

Bengat Homestead 1917

It is the third year of the Great War, and sixteen men and boys born in this village have fallen. Because their earthly remains are absent from the graveyard, Isabella of Bengat homestead keeps count of them in her head. It is not hard to do. In spite of her seventy years, Isabella can name every one of the three hundred sixty-three people who call Rosenau home. She can name their parents, their godparents, and their grandparents, with first names, family names, and clan names. She could tell some secrets, but she doesn't. Isabella has felt the bite of old age for some time now, but this war is worse. Day by day she feels its weight wearing her own secrets thin, transparent. Wringing them dry.

Three soldiers have come home from the battlefields for good, drifting in like ghosts set on retribution. Every Sunday, this Sunday, they put themselves on display at church. Fellele's Jodok coughs through the mass, his lungs giving way bit by bit like rotted cheesecloth. His brother Michel—born on the same day as her own son, forty-two years ago, the two of them the oldest to be sent away to fight—is all but deaf. He shows no other outward sign of injury, but his eyes have something small and sour about them; they put Isabella in mind of blighted apples. Cobbler's Manuel has lost the use of his right arm. After mass Isabella hears Manuel tell a neighbor that on his farmstead he is as useful as the tits on the boar. His tone, jovial and desperate, makes Isabella shudder.

There are three men still gone, one fighting in the South Tirol. Two others, including Isabella's Peter, are in Galicia. They have had no news of Peter in four months. Now the whole household—Isabella, Alois, and their widowed daughter, Barbara, as well as Peter's wife and four children—lives with an ear turned toward the road. They wait for the sound of his step, or for word that he has fallen. The weight of this, all of them leaning toward the road, seems to have tipped the family out of balance and set them spinning haphazardly. They are moons of a missing planet.

Peter's wife is the worst, lopsided and wobbling ever more out of control. Anna seldom does her chores, she rarely sits down to table, and she has stopped coming to church. Now, after mass, Isabella makes excuses for her daughter-in-law, but the truth burns bright on her face.

At Sunday dinner Alois talks about the latest requisition order from the war office: the military now wants all the wool, even from the sheep less than two years old. Barbara clucks at this; distress makes her noisy, but Isabella takes in the bad news without a word of protest. She is watching her grandchildren eat, making sure every spoonful of precious broth and meat gets into them. Alois has slaughtered a goat in the dark of night, without notifying the authorities. The children must have something, they reason, young boys and a teenage girl—even if it is at the expense of their father on the line.

When dinner is over, Isabella goes out into the *Schopf*. It is unseasonably warm for early March. Isabella knows without looking that the crocuses have poked up their noses; she knows too that winter is not done.

Anna is sitting on the step with Peter's guitar in her lap. The others are taking Sunday afternoon naps, Barbara in her little attic room, Alois stretched out against the warmth of the tile oven in the *Stube*. Isabella is tired, but she settles down next to her daughter-in-law. She wants to say something that will do more good than harm. She feels full-up with words, crowded with them, a belly bloated with words; but still the right ones dance away from her. A blunt scythe can be whetted, Isabella thinks, but unwilling words are eternally dull.

Down at the bottom of the garden there is a pear tree that has always been a favorite with the children. Its lowest branches form a cradle at the trunk, and Isabella sees that her granddaughter has claimed that spot for her nap. Long legs in gray woolen stockings peek out from the sweeping curves of tucked-up skirts and underskirts. Her hair is a mahogany waterfall flowing to her waist. She is half asleep, head thrown back against the trunk, her neck arched at an angle that reminds Isabella of a fish leaping joyously in midstream.

"What a sight she is," Anna murmurs, surprising Isabella so that she jumps a little. Anna turns toward her, insistent. "Don't you think?"

"A-yo." Isabella nods. "A-yo. A comely child."

Appeased, Anna turns her attention to the knobby white fingers of the Praying Hands. Her own hands rest over the bridge of the guitar as they once rested on the rounded form of her pregnancies.

Isabella clears her throat. "It has always seemed strange to me that folks like to talk of womanly beauty—"

"You would notice that," Anna interrupts. Isabella does not take offense; the years have worn away the homely-woman wariness with which she paced out her youth.

"–and how little they talk about the beauty of men," Isabella finishes.

This strikes Anna silent; she knows now the subject is Peter.

"Oh, our Olga is a pleasure to look at. But I have never seen a woman so fair as a young man in the early days of his full strength." And Isabella falters, because she cannot say out loud what is in her mind: *when he is not yet able to put a face on death.*

Her daughters had been good, biddable girls, eager to please and hardworking and spirited. On Saturday nights they had crowded around the washbasin and uncovered the white skin of their shoulders, their narrow backs, their round breasts. Isabella had noted, with pride and considerable discomfort, that they were well favored. This she kept to herself, superstitiously, fearing for the completeness of these beings she had somehow conjured out of her own flesh. On the day her Luise married–Isabella relives this memory now, painfully–she had been resolved to say that word, that overused but magical word that lives in the eternity between *not beautiful* and *not plain*. In the end she had put her hands on Luise's shoulders and looked into her eyes to say, "Handsome is as handsome does."

To her daughter-in-law, a woman who has possessed beauty, and possesses some of it still in a careless and unwitting way, Isabella can now say those things that she could not say to her own daughters when they were young. "At Olga's age, at seventeen, Peter was the most beautiful creature, man or animal, that God ever put on this earth."

Anna jerks in surprise; her cuff buttons catch on the strings of the guitar and play a jagged chord when she pulls them free.

"I used to send him to the village on nonsense errands, just to watch him run," Isabella tells her. "His legs! When he married you my main unhappiness was not being able to send him on errands anymore. There!" Isabella laughs a little, ill at ease. "I've shocked you with my secrets."

"That's not much of a secret," Anna says, but her voice has taken on some life; she leans toward Isabella. "Anybody with eyes in their head could see that for himself, how you feel about your boy."

Isabella swallows hard. "Here you are expecting me to give you a lecture about duty and fortitude in the face of loss, and instead I tell you things you know already."

Anxiety blossoms suddenly on Anna's face and she opens her mouth to protest the idea of loss, but her words are cut off by a flurry in the pear tree: Olga is gathering her skirts to leap to the ground. Now she is headed toward them at a trot, her vision trained on the road that leads to the homestead from above and behind. Isabella sits up, alarmed as Olga breaks into a run, yelling, pointing, because something, someone, is headed toward them and Olga has seen who it is. A cool fear begins to breathe on the back of Isabella's neck as she takes in the sound of hoofbeats on the dirt road. The skin rises on her arms; she can feel each hair stand up as the courier—who has ridden here four twisty uphill kilometers on a Sunday afternoon—rounds the corner.

The guitar falls down the steps with a discordant crash as Anna stands. The courier dismounts and the mailbag thumps against his leg; Isabella imagines that she can hear him breathing. Anna has one hand pressed against her throat and the other on her mouth, half muffling a high keening wail.

He reaches into his bag. With Anna's wail still hanging in the air, the women stand, dazed, looking at this stranger who has never before come to their door. They stare at his arm extended like a blade from underneath the wool cape, its long dark length, and on his flat palm, bloodless white, the telegram, upside down. Its back is stained with dried rain, scattered like pox marks. The women stand like this for two, three, four heartbeats, and then Olga rushes up, breathless, and snatches the telegram away from the courier; she holds it face up: it is not edged in black. She holds it up over her head so that her grandfather and brothers and aunt, who have come out on the *Schopf* behind Isabella and Anna, can see this too: *it is not edged in black.* Then, still breathing hard, she hands it to her mother, who sits down heavily, and with pale rough hands opens the envelope to read that Peter is alive, that he has lost a leg, an unspecified number of fingers, and an eye, and that he is recovered enough now to be fetched home.

First with child at the age of twenty-four, Isabella had wished herself a son but bore a daughter. She was anxious, having no experience of sisters, and only her own uneasy girlself to measure things by: she had been small and round and plain as a day-old loaf of brown bread. But Luise, like Margit to come after her, took after Alois: long and bony, with spindly fingers and toes; this set Isabella's mind at ease. She gave everything affectionate she could find in herself to her girls, and in time she came to the belief that a woman must have a daughter to rest easy in her grave.

   Then Peter was born, and Isabella fell into a new kind of devotion, awash in an unexpected energy that made her arms quiver and her fingers jerk. She realized, with some guilt but no regret, that she had been holding back the quick of herself, the bloody beat of her heart, for a son. For Peter. It took her a long time, too long, to find some balance, to show an interest in the girls again. Even then, when no one was looking, she would pick Peter up and draw in his scent. She chided herself for taking such pleasure in his smell, even as she ran her nose over the crown of his scalp, pink and firm and fuzzy as a peach but much sweeter. She would fit her lower face to his small one, her nose buried in the soft folds between ear and shoulder, and inhale until she was dizzy. She did this until he was too old to tolerate it, and then she mourned the loss.

   Now Isabella spends as much time as she can spare at

the window watching Peter, who spends his days whittling in the *Schopf* with the shutters propped up to let in the light. She tells herself that he doesn't know about this habit of hers.

Peter sits with the damaged side of his face bared to the mild winter sun. Like a blessing, the sunlight strokes what his mother cannot bring herself to look at: it moves tenderly over the mass of scar tissue that ripples from his hairline down the left side of his face to puddle on what was once a smooth cheek, a well-formed ear, a clean jaw. It soaks deep into the patch that hides the empty eye socket.

Isabella watches Peter as he turns his one eye and his mind, still whole and sharp, to the piece of wood wedged against his right thigh. Beneath his blade a world has come to life. A meadow of flowers twists and twirls around the long, tapered shaft of wood. Half hidden in a mass of blossoms, a stag raises his head. There are birds, squirrels, ibexes, and he is working now on a small group of marmots.

Quietly, the youngest of his boys slips into the *Schopf* to sit with his father. Peter makes no move to discourage him, but he pulls his cap down low over the left side of his face. Shavings still fall in fragile tendrils from the point of his knife. Isabella listens as Peter and Leo talk. Leo is seven, and so in love with his father that his ruined face is no penance at all. They talk about the marmots, who live in the highest ranges and cut grass and spread it to dry on rocks in the sun, using the sweet hay to build nests in their burrows. Leo imitates the high warning whistle the marmots make to their young, and Peter laughs out loud; Isabella feels her insides clutching. She chides herself for her weakness, for her jealousy of a seven-year-old child.

When Peter puts aside his knife, Isabella turns away quickly. She will not watch her son take up his wooden prosthesis, now covered to the hinged knee with flowers and vines and animals, and strap it to the stump where his left leg used to be.

* * *

It is four weeks since Alois went to bring their son home. From the first day Peter has refused to be an invalid, to stay in bed, to be nursed. Instead, he sits out in the *Schopf* whenever the weather will allow, carving a forest into a leg.

In those four weeks, Isabella has dreamed of her son every night. In her dreams she touches him, softly, lovingly, but even so his scars peel open under her palms, the flesh parting drained and cold to show her his skull, bluish white. Isabella wakes up hiccuping in fright, her hands clenched to her heart, trying to calm the madness thudding there.

Now, in April, the winter has raised its voice again. For sixty years weather has not kept Isabella away from mass, every Wednesday and Sunday, and she will not give in this morning. There are things to pray for. It is just dawn when she wraps herself in her winter cloak of heavy boiled wool, and works the horn buttons that are a misery to her achy joints. Her feet, swaddled in more wool, slide around inside an old pair of Alois's boots. These days they are too swollen for anything smaller.

Together Barbara and Isabella start down the mountainside to the village. They must stop every ten minutes to let Isabella catch her breath. She knocks snow from her boots with impatient taps of her walking stick, leaning on Barbara. Isabella is glad to have her youngest daughter with her when she goes to mass. Barbara is a seventeen-year widow, and that burden sits heavy. She will never marry again; there are no men to marry. Isabella goes to mass to make the Lord take note of her losses.

In the village they stop before mass to buy flour and salt and cornmeal. Barbara counts out precious coins onto the counter in front of Grumpy Marie, her lips moving silently. The ration cards, even more precious, she takes out of their hiding place in her bodice.

There are many women in the shop, and they are whispering among themselves; from their tone alone Isabella knows that something has happened which both horrifies and pleases them. She drags Barbara away before they can load her down with anybody else's sorrow. She is thinking about this, about the scarcity of linen, sugar, lard, tea, and the surplus of sorrow, as she follows her daughter down the path and into the church square. Isabella is so focused on the ice underfoot that she bumps into Barbara, not realizing that she has stopped. There on the edge of the square Isabella looks up and sees what has brought them to a halt.

Miller's Theres, twenty years old and the tenth of eleven children, slightly built but a hard worker, has been put into stocks in the middle of the square and left for the village to mock. On either side of her head, bare hands protude from the rough holes. Her mouth hangs open, and she heaves for breath like a dog in the summer sun. There is a dark bruise on her jaw. Her hair is a mat of straw and muck, set off by a light dusting of snow. Around her neck hangs a cast-off piece of wood on which someone has scrawled one word in red paint, in peaks and angles so sharp that Isabella need not even squint to read it: *Whore.* She is so startled at this sight that she cannot take it in all at once. It seems to her that the girl is wearing a mask, and then she realizes that Theres's cheeks are covered with dirt and ice, and that tears still run from her closed eyes.

Suddenly tired, more than tired, Isabella wants to turn and go home, but there are people behind them, pressing forward to get into the square. Barbara takes her mother's hand, and Isabella lets herself be pulled away; they edge in a wide arc toward the church. Barbara holds Isabella's arm as they climb the steps to the door. Later, Isabella cannot say what made her turn, but she does turn now, and from this vantage point she sees it all.

There is a crowd of men around Theres. Isabella recognizes the Wainwright, and Half-Moon Hollow's Bartle, and a half dozen men who have lost sons or brothers or nephews on the line. Between them, shackled, is a prisoner of war. Like Theres, he is bareheaded, but he holds his head up. This strikes Isabella, the way he holds up his chin, the way he looks around, as if he were a tourist here and considering moving on.

Then the Wainwright steps forward to pull the girl's head up by the hair, baring her neck as if for the butcher's knife. The crowd is suddenly quiet, and the Wainwright's voice carries as he rants at her, shaking her head back and forth. If she sees the prisoner they push in front of her, she gives no sign of it. She is blank, her icy face reflecting back the winter sky and nothing human. This enrages the Wainwright. His voice hacks at her. He lets go of her hair so that he can kick her in the legs, the ribs, hunching over her, prodding her, his face red and his eyes wild with fury. There is a loud cry, and another: the girl's mother screams and screams again and then falls still.

Barbara gasps and reaches blindly for her own mother. Isabella turns toward her, knowing that she must go now, or swoon. And so she doesn't see the scuffle; she looks up into sudden confusion in the square and sees the Wainwright sprawled on the ground. It takes a second more to realize that the soldier is free, and that he is running. He dodges easily away when arms reach out toward him. With a graceful leap he clears a fence, and with that he is gone, out of the crowd. As he runs, his darkness, his foreignness, stand out against the snowy field.

Isabella watches him, sees his arms pumping, his legs working, the muscles of his calves straining against the cheap material of the striped trousers. Isabella watches him run and she rejoices in the sight.

In the evening, when the children are in bed, the adults sit together.

Alois comes in from checking the livestock, bringing with him the warm, oversweet smell of cow flesh, the counterpoint scent of his pipe tobacco, the spark of new snow. His cheeks are ruddy with the cold, and without warning, Isabella remembers the winter evening when she was twenty-two and she came with her brother Kaspar to a dance party at Bengat homestead. Here in this very room, the furniture moved aside. There had been singing, and a dulcimer and guitar, and a quarter-moon like a new scythe gliding over the peaks of the Three Sisters. And there had been Bengat's Alois, strong and bright as that moon, watched with secret eyes by every single girl except Isabella. She had had no hopes of him, or of herself.

"That was the night you first took note of me," Isabella says now to Alois, pulling him into the sudden flow of her memories. She sounds like a rambling old woman, she knows this even without Barbara's concerned and uneasy stare. But Alois is not surprised at this feat she demands of him; after all these years he can find his wife without signposts.

"Better ice that melts than fire that goes out," Alois says, smiling.

Isabella nods, for this is the simple truth of marriage.

Alois settles into his chair, but he doesn't reach, as he usually does, for the *Farmer's Weekly*. Tonight they need no news of the outside world.

"He was a Russian," Alois begins. "They had him on the crew laying the new road down at Muddy Bend."

"There at the mill." Peter says out loud what each is thinking. He has stretched out on the warming bench that rounds the tiled oven. His injured side is turned in to rest against the sleek glazed tiles, the wooden leg at an angle, bent at the knee to let the heel rest on the bench. The lamplight plays over the leaves and flowers, making them flicker. Anna sits at Peter's head with her knitting in her lap.

"The miller's womenfolk have been feeding the crew mornings and middays, must be for months now, since it got real cold."

Barbara draws breath through her teeth as if she feels this cold herself.

Anna lets her knitting rest in her lap as her fingers stray toward Peter, brushing lightly against his hair. Peter catches her hand and holds it against his good cheek.

"Where could he have been running to?" Anna murmurs.

"Home," Peter says. "He was running home."

Isabella looks away from them and out the window; the snow keeps on, remorseless, and the oil lamp reflects white and white again in the gently waving panes of glass that separate this room from the night. In the blank reflection Isabella sees the young soldier, his dark hair and mustache, his arms and shoulders ropy with muscle, his hands curved for all time to the shape of the sledgehammer's shaft. She imagines him with the girl, his loneliness washed away for a little while, the homesickness and misery banished in the face of different desires, hurried and rare. The girl is faceless behind her mask of frozen tears; she doesn't matter. No, it is the soldier Isabella thinks of, whole and healthy, with strong legs pushing, pushing. Pushing him into the girl, then pushing him away, pumping as he runs through the snow.

She almost hears the shot again, it is that real to her. There is a clatter as the basket of wool falls from her lap to the floor. Barbara is looking at her, eyes tight with fear, as Isabella stands and spreads her apron flat with her hands.

"Mama?"

"Bella?" Alois echoes as Isabella walks across the room and stops in front of Peter.

Isabella goes down on her knees next to her son, her bones snapping and protesting, but she goes down anyway. There is a rustle as Anna moves away, but Isabella takes no note of this; she puts her hand on her son, her right palm on the ruined left side of his face, to turn him full toward her, to meet his eyes. He has been waiting for her all these days, all these weeks: he has been patient. But there is something of wariness, some caution in his eyes as well; Isabella sees this now and it makes her cringe. She runs her fingers–gently, gently–over the waves of flesh, red and purple; she traces the thick seams the doctors left behind; she cups his sunken cheek in her own seamed palm. There is murmuring around her: Alois, Anna, Barbara's voice rising shrill. Only Peter is quiet. Peter doesn't protest or turn away, and this gives her the strength to stay.

He smells of linseed ointment, of pipe tobacco and wood sap, of his wife and his union with her–this gives Isabella pause, but only for a moment. She draws in his smell and now she finds him again, the boy he was, a boy running bare-legged down the road while his mother watches at the window. When his arm comes up and around her shoulder, Isabella slides her fingers into her son's hair, puts her face to the hollow between ear and shoulder, and draws in a breath.

Angelika

Bent Elbow Homestead 1920

The farmer provides good milk; the natural consequence of good milk is good cheese. There's no cheese without rennet and no good cheese with poor rennet, and so there's a skill to it, you see.

There's things you must have to make your rennet: a piece of the fourth stomach of a suckling calf, one that's had naught but milk and the curd. Salt. Yolk of four eggs. Three, if they are large. A measure of sweet cream, thick enough to hold a spoon upright. Strong brine, with saxifrage steeped in it.

Listen now and I'll tell you the secret of any good farm woman. She may keep the homestead and children above all reproach; but her cheese is her true judge.

This is what you must do to ensure good rennet: Wait until the moon is waxing. Braid your hair tight, and cover it well. Fold back your sleeves properly. Say a Hail Mary and in your prayer remember Saints Barnabus and Bartholomew. Then scrub your hands in hot water and vinegar, and remember this: if you are slovenly, if you do not take care to work with clean bowls and spoons and cloths, then the saints cannot help you and you will have reason to fear when the wheel is taken from the press.

A farmer's wife is as good as her cheese; her cheese can be no better than her rennet. Many other failings may stay hid throughout the years: she can feed unrisen bread to the sow and cut up the misbegotten needlework for cleaning rags and bury children her womb refuses to nourish in the dark corners of the garden. Her husband will never be the wiser, if she does not tell him. It is easy to feed him silence, at the kitchen table and even in his own bed: he may suspect, but what can he know?

But there is no place for a woman to hide her cheese.

He will take it from the press to put it before her, and it will tell its own tale: poor of grain, and the rennet was weak; too tough, and the curd was broke too soon; too soft, the whey was not pressed clean out; hoven, the curd underworked; dry, too much of the cream skimmed off; studded with a single hair, and there is no excuse or explanation. Our faults—impatience, laziness, greed, sloth—all come to the light in the round disks of pale gold, in the cool damp dimness of the cheese cellar. Where you face your imperfections, with a man as witness who is first a farmer and maybe, sometime else, a husband.

Barbara

Bengat Homestead 1921

Wrung clean out after a day walking behind the hay tedder, Alois worries out loud that the missing pitchfork might be in the upper loft. So Barbara goes to have a look, thinking her father will rest easier once that fork has found its way home. And that's where she finds them, her niece Olga and Olga's beau, out of most of their clothes already and dizzy on the brink of perdition. They are so lost in each other that they don't notice Barbara until she is up the ladder and standing in front of them, close enough to see the hay dust circling their heads in unruly halos, their faces branded with slanting thrusts of sunlight.

Now, Goat-Cheese Willi's Klaus has the common sense to be ashamed: those parts of him that aren't browned by the sun color up and he turns away. But Olga, Barbara's Olga comes up on her knees in the hay to look at her aunt, bared breasts stung red not with embarrassment but with defiance.

From the *Schopf,* where she is carding wool with measured, twisting swipes of the combs, Barbara watches Klaus sprint away down the mountainside. Her palms are slick with lanolin; from between the combs, a cloud of wool froths up like the thinning hair of an old woman.

Olga comes to Barbara in quick, sure steps. Her feet are dusty with hay. She still has that look about her; she is resolute. What she has to tell Barbara is what she believes to be true.

"Aunt Barbara," Olga says calmly, her chin tilted up, only her whisper giving away her worry. "You don't know what it's like to be in love."

What Barbara doesn't know is where to look with her disappointment. Olga's guile stings, but it is her sincerity, her absolute faith in Barbara's ignorance, that draws blood. It is true that Barbara is forty-six years old and that she has been widowed now for all of Olga's twenty-one years. It is true that her bed is as empty and comfortless as a church on a rainy Monday morning. But she has not forgotten about love. What it was like.

"I was crazy in love myself, once," she tells her niece, her hurt showing plain. It seems to Barbara that it is time to tell Olga about Franz Michel, but before she can think how to start, Olga leans over and puts her smooth cheek against Barbara's.

"Please, Auntie," she says now, melting into what she has been hiding all along, what she always will be to Barbara, who helped her mama bring her into the world: a little girl. "Please."

And Barbara sighs and nods and strokes Olga's head with its crown of dark braids, so much like her own in those days when she was young enough to take love for granted.

Barbara's Franz Michel had been a carpenter: he had strong, blunt hands with fingers thick as rope, but still he had the touch, for wood, for animal flesh, for woman flesh. He had started courting Barbara in the fall, and by the time spring came around Isabella was worried enough to quote Saint Paul. "It is better to marry than to burn," she would say to Barbara when Alois wasn't within hearing. Barbara remembers those words, how they ran through her head on her wedding night, and how wicked she felt when she found out she could have both: she had married, and still Franz Michel set her to burning. Franz Michel, who could turn a table leg to last a hundred years, could turn her inside out, and himself too in the process.

That same summer Barbara's brother Peter had married his Anna; the following spring Olga was born, and on the morning after her baptism Franz Michel climbed up onto the barn roof to mend some shingles, lost his footing, and fell on his head. A week after the burial Barbara packed up her belongings, taking with her only what she had brought to Half-Moon Hollow as a bride: her clothes, her linen and featherbeds, some crockery, three ewes, and a ram. She left the rest to Franz Michel's brother Bartle, who had never thought he'd be in a position to marry, and was taken by surprise when the homestead was suddenly his. Bartle sent along with her the third-best cow, in way of compensation for her trouble and the loss of Franz Michel.

Alois came to fetch her back to Bengat. Barbara sat next to her father on the buckboard, her shoulders set stiff toward Half-Moon Hollow, not looking to the left or right. Through the village without a glance at the women on their way up the church steps for mass, the same women who had danced at her wedding party. The same church where she had been married. Passing the graveyard gate, she could see the high mound of dark earth, the cross wreathed with a black banner. A married man in his final resting place.

Breathless, Barbara had asked to get out, and then jumped down before Alois could bring the wagon to a halt. She needed to feel her feet under her, the gravel of the hard-packed road on her heels. Her throat burning with swallowed tears, she stood watching her father plod on. The cow swayed along after the wagon.

He thinks I'm going to the grave, Barbara thought.

And he was right. She must go to Franz Michel's grave today and every time she went to mass and every time she came into the village, because she was a widow and her husband had fled from her into one kind of purgatory and left her to another.

Barbara stood there looking back toward Half-Moon Hollow, where she had lived for just over a year, where she had been the farmer's wife, where she had thought to live out her life and bear her children and die. Then she looked up toward Bengat, the house leaning out over the cliff. Her mother's household, and after that, when one day her mother was gone, her sister-in-law Anna's.

But there was nowhere else to go, and so she climbed the path to Bengat and let herself be taken in.

The only surprise waiting for her was the sheep: her father said they were hers, in her charge. Whatever profit came of them belonged to her, and when she married again she would have a dowry any farmer would be glad of. Barbara tried to look surprised at the idea of marrying again, ashamed of the fact that this thought had come to her almost as soon as Franz Michel died. Before the last of his blood had been soaked out of her apron.

She waited five years before showing any interest, and then found little in return. In spite of the sheep, now grown to a fine number, in spite of the money she had put aside. Cobbler's Manuel took some note and would have made a wife of her, but his older brother got their homestead and there was no place to set up housekeeping. He came courting every Sunday for years, making a fool of himself for a hopeless match. Barbara grew impatient with him when she saw he would never find the courage to do more than hold her hand, even when they went off to walk in the darkened woods and watch the night sky. Still, Manuel came courting: in the spring when the Bengat folks went to *Vorschaß*, he would walk up to Little Calf Lake to sit with her: two hours each way to hold her hand for an hour, every Sunday.

Then the war came along and took all the men. The few who came back were ruined for good but got wives anyway. Manuel was one of them, but there was still no land and no hope of a homestead and nothing to give Barbara, and so he married the innkeeper's widow, kept two cows, and poured beer with his lame arm pinned to his side. Other women took hired men from far off, or went into service in the flatlands and married there, or turned inward, folded inward on themselves, gave up wearing the white linen sleeves of maidens, and learned to answer to "spinster."

When Barbara saw that she wasn't going to get a second chance, she settled in at Bengat. For all these years she has been a good daughter, a support to her brother and his wife, another pair of hands in the kitchen, and a strong back in the barn and hayfield. She is as reliable and invisible as any maiden aunt. As if Barbara had never had a cookstove or chickens or a garden to call her own. As if Franz Michel had never taken her home to Half-Moon Hollow and showed her the hidden, curious needs of men, or the shape of desire.

When Anna comes back from trading in the village on Saturday morning, she puts the money purse in the cupboard where it has always made its home and she sits down at the kitchen table. Barbara's thumbs are stained with the plums she is pitting; she is surrounded by a fortress of glittering canning jars. Out at the clothesline Olga is pummeling the good carpet, and Anna taps her finger on the tabletop to the the steady *whack*

whack whack of the rug beater. Barbara thinks of the dust swirling around Olga. Wrapping around her. And she puts the thought away, out of Anna's view.

"Where's Jakob?" Anna asks suddenly.

Barbara looks up. "I thought he went down the village with you."

"Lord amighty." Anna gets up and opens the kitchen window to lean out, the heel of one hand braced on the frame. "Leo!" she calls. "Tony!" And then as Leo runs toward her from the woodpile: "Go after your little brother!"

"He headed for Bent Elbow, Mama?"

"Where else?" She flaps her apron at him impatiently. "That child will wander," she mutters, turning away from the window.

Jakob, three years old and curious unto death, is devoted to Bent Elbow's Martha, a fey dark-eyed child one year older than he is himself; he sets off in her direction when the mood takes him. This summer they have brought him back once a week at least. There was a time when Barbara would have doubted a three-year-old could walk all that way, but Jakob has showed her an otherworldly determination that she must respect. Barbara is thinking about Jakob, about his wandering tendencies. He sometimes goes off in the night, which is something that she knows but Anna doesn't, because it is a secret need, a weakness, that Barbara shares with him. When she looks up, Barbara sees Anna watching her.

"What?" she asks.

"The Wainwright is getting married," Anna says, and then her back is turned as she changes her apron and sets to work on dinner.

Barbara concentrates on the task before her: the smooth, taut skin of the plum, a deep color beyond purple but glinting with hidden greens and yellows. The knife slices to the heart.

She slips her thumb along the keen edge of the pit and under it; as the pale flesh gives up the stone, it whispers and tears. Barbara blinks hard at the sound.

"Is he?"

"Just as quick as the banns can be spoken. Miller's Theres."

Barbara puts down her knife. "Imagine," she says to her stained fingers.

"A-yo," says Anna, grim. "A girl he beat on the church square in sight of God and man, just four years ago."

"Who would have thought?" murmurs Barbara.

"Not me," Anna agrees. "Not after that shameful episode. What is she thinking, to marry the Wainright, I want to know. What is her mama thinking, to let her?"

When Barbara has nothing to say to this, Anna sighs.

"Anyways, she wouldn't give her word till he promised to get the twins out of the house. Said she didn't want to be looking after cripples. Wainwright claims he's going to put things to rights at River's Bend and set them up down there. Stante will come work same as before, and he'll get a wage and provisions."

"Don't expect Grumpy Marie's going to take up house-keeping at River's Bend," says Barbara, studying a bruise on the plum in her hand.

Anna laughs hoarsely. "Not likely she'd give up being postmistress. No, she'll stay at the homeplace and make her peace with a new stepmother, I suppose. There's a woman from Ackenau who's willing to come up and look after Michel, do the cooking and cleaning. From that homestead on the Low Road, you know the one, where they keep that bad-tempered one-horned bull."

Anna pauses, her elbows tucked into her sides. "They are my nephews and I have always wanted them here, but they are young men now. River's Bend is theirs by rights. They need a place of their own."

"Of course they do."

The women listen to the carpet beater thumping like a heart.

Barbara says, "I think I'll go to the village after dinner and attend to the graves."

"I thought you might want to." Anna nods.

At the table Alois cannot get over the news. Since his Isabella died and Peter and the boys have taken over most of the work, Alois finds it hard to stay interested in things, but the Wainwright has always prickled him the wrong way.

"Well," he says. "Ignaz has finally found a wife. It must be twenty years since Old Woman passed on." Alois may not be the only one who remembers that the Wainwright was once baptized and has a calling-name, but he is the only one who handles it.

"Daddy, think on it," Barbara chides softly. "It's closer to thirty years."

"Thirty years to find a wife!" says Alois. "Well, I suppose he aimed too high to start with. Running after young girls when a widow woman would have done the job." He winks at Barbara and she smiles grimly into her soup bowl.

"That's a point," Peter says. "Just now I'm wondering why the Wainwright never came to call on you, Bärbele, when he went after just about every other unmarried woman in the village." But he smiles at her as he says this, and that little smile, kindly meant, pushes Barbara further than she wants to go.

"Unmarried is right. He's never showed interest in widow women," Barbara says quietly, her eyes averted. "Though there's enough of us around since the war."

"The tried-and-true couldn't interest him," says Alois. "He wanted a young girl, a virgin."

"Ha!" Olga sniffs. "And look what he got instead. One that's been tried, true enough." Then, self-conscious, she glances at Barbara and has the good grace to blush.

Anna jerks her head at her daughter, displeased. "Olga," she snaps. "Shame on you for such talk. Scandalmongering."

"What's a scandal?" asks Jakob. His morning jaunt toward Bent Elbow has made him hungry, and he talks with his mouth full of cheese fritters, overlooking his mother's frown.

"A scandal is when a man close to seventy marries a twenty-five-year-old woman," says Peter.

"A woman with a weakness for Russian prisoners of war," Alois adds.

Anna puts down her spoon. "The girl made a mistake once, and now she's made a choice. That's her business and none of ours. And I won't have you all leaving compassion and charity behind on the church pew."

"Your mother is right, children," Peter says, reaching for the salad bowl. "You can chew on gossip all day long, but it will never put meat on your bones."

In the afternoon Barbara loads the pushcart with the tools she will need to tend the graves, and sets off with Jakob trotting beside her. He is a quiet child and leaves her to her thoughts as long as she lets him explore.

When her work at the graves is done—weeding, watering, pruning, a hasty rosary—Barbara washes her hands in the fountain and dries them on her apron. Then she calls Jakob to her side and heads toward the Wainwright's. Her heart is pounding; she feels the color mounting on her cheeks. Blame it on the heat, she tells herself. She sends Jakob to the smithy to sit with his cousin Stante.

The Wainwright is alone in the shop. Barbara had been expecting Grumpy Marie behind the counter and is surprised at her good luck in finding him instead. He nods at her and raises a single eyebrow.

"I need a half kilo of cooking salt," Barbara says, putting her basket to rest on the floor.

While the Wainwright weighs out the salt, Barbara turns to look at the stacks of fabric, the colors and patterns blurring together in an agitated jumble.

"Here you are, then," he says to her back.

"There's something else." She turns to meet his gaze. "I come by to congratulate you on your upcoming marriage. The sister-in-law brought the news up to Bengat earlier."

"So people are talking," he says, sticking out his lower lip. "Do I look like I care?"

Barbara studies him. At almost seventy he still has a full head of dark hair, slightly curly over a high forehead freckled with age. In his profile there is still a lot of the handsome man he was once, in spite of his teeth. He grins at her suddenly, as if to show off their imperfections.

"Come on now, Babele," he says, in a wheedling voice she has only heard from him in the half-light of the moon. "You can't expect anything else."

Barbara watches the discomfort growing on his face as she lets her silence do its work. She watches him, and she thinks of all the women who have refused to marry him: the spinster ladies, women who never found husbands because there weren't enough men or enough land to go around, or because they were bred to be workers and brought up to be daughters and didn't know how to be anything else. The Wainwright had approached them, but every single one of them had preferred the trouble they knew intimately, the demands of spinsterhood, the hazy anxieties of celibacy, the dependency on brothers and fathers, to a mean old man in their beds.

"Well, Ignaz," she says finally, softly. "You're wrong this time. There is something I expect from you. I want to move into the River's Bend homestead with the twins, to look after them."

"I already made arrangements," he says quietly, but his eyes jump nervously around the room.

"Unmake them, then."

"That would be hard," the Wainwright says, running a hand over the bristle on his chin.

"It would be a sight harder if I was to ask your bride instead of you, give her some background."

His eyes narrow. "It's your reputation," he says. "You are mighty reckless with it."

Barbara smiles for the first time. "I was crazy in love once, Ignaz, don't you know. Maybe I'm crazier out of it, but it seems to me I got nothing to lose. This is my last chance for a home of my own."

She can see the calculations moving behind his eyes, the additions and subtractions, the troubles and the profits weighed and measured.

He shrugs. "You can't prove nothing."

Barbara feels a rush of heat to her face as she leans over the counter toward him. The smells on him, tobacco and peppermint and leather, hone her words to sharp points.

"Now, maybe I'd be willing to invest something in the fixing up of River's Bend," she says. "Something I been saving for fifteen years."

There is a light of sudden interest in his eyes. "What," he says hoarsely, "you willing to sell your sheep?"

"No, I got something here you gave me, Ignaz, in your affection, so I knew they must be valuable. Thought this might come in handy some day."

She ignores his puzzled expression and takes a sack from her marketing basket. With slow, methodical movements she unties the string and slowly upends the sack. A wave of pale yellow hard candy rattles out, each wrapped in a twist of paper; a few fall on the counter.

"Count them," she says. "There's three hundred and forty-three of them. That comes to somewhere around two a month for fifteen years, taking into account I was away at *Vorschaß* for a good eight weeks in the spring and fall."

His confusion lasts only a moment. "What," he says, lifting his chin defensively, "you couldn't have bought these sweets for yourself?"

"Maybe I did," she says. Barbara is relieved to discover how easy it is to outthink him; still her fingers tremble, so she puts them deep in her apron pockets. "Why don't we call Marie down here and see if she remembers ever once in her entire life selling me a single sourball."

He is beat now, and she sees this on his face and in his stiffened shoulders.

"What do you want from me?"

She smiles again. "I want living privileges at River's Bend for the rest of my life. I want the place fixed up proper. I want decent provisions, every week. I'll look after the boys, don't worry. That will be my pleasure."

"I can't afford all that!"

"Yes, you can. She gets her payment up front. I been lifting my skirt for you in dark corners for fifteen years, and I will take my payment now. It's the cost of a young woman in your bed, Ignaz. You can afford it fine."

He leans on the counter. There is a dry grinding and the sudden smell of lemon as a sourball is crushed under the weight of his palm. "But what will folks think?" he whispers.

"It's a little late to worry about that, Ignaz," Barbara says impatiently. "You should of thought of that when you decided I was too old to marry. But never worry. Folks will think that you suddenly learned the value of generosity. That you are finally taking a real interest in the comfort and welfare of your grandsons." And she laughs as she picks up her basket and turns to go.

"Folks will never believe that!" he sputters.

Barbara glances back at him from the door. "You're right," she says, still laughing, and she leaves him there hunched over the evidence of his miserly regard, and her own desperation.

Klaus is gone from the village the next two Sundays, off to the lowlands to deliver his father's goat cheese; when he finally comes courting again, he sits in the *Stube* and keeps up a conversation with Peter and Anna as though he never had his hands on their only daughter. As if he didn't have his hands on her now, under the table. Barbara tries not to look up from her spinning, because when she does she sees how Klaus uses his thumb to draw circles on Olga's exposed palm so that her fingers, slightly curled, twitch gently.

"So tell me again how this works," Alois is saying to Barbara. "I don't understand what would move the Wainwright to put running water and a toilet into River's Bend."

"Maybe he's feeling guilty," Peter suggests. "About Stante and Michel, how he's treated them all these years."

Anna glances at Barbara, whose attention does not waver from the spindle. "He's got enough to feel guilty about, that's true," Anna says. "But guilt don't come natural to the Wainwright."

Klaus clears his throat a couple of times into a sudden silence. "Well, guilty or not, he's getting married on Tuesday and there's a wedding party Tuesday night."

"True enough," says Peter slowly. He turns to look at his sister. "That very day our Barbara will be taking leave of the family." He leans over and pats his wife's knee. "Can you get on without her?" he says playfully.

Anna smiles. "Why, I suppose I must, though we will miss her. She'll just be on the other side of the village, though, won't she?"

Finally Barbara looks up. There is something in her face that Anna understands but the men don't see: she is struggling to put away her resentment.

Peter turns to Klaus. "You planning on showing your face at that wedding party?"

"I thought I might," says Klaus. He pauses, and when Peter doesn't help him along, he flushes. "I thought I might walk Olga down to the Eagle," he says. "If that suits you." Klaus looks at Peter, at Alois, then at her mama, then at Barbara. Barbara decides that she must admire him, after all: he is a likely young man, strong in body and in spirit, strong enough to stand up to the reproach Barbara could hand him, strong enough to deal with Olga.

Peter adjusts his eye patch as he looks hard at Klaus. Jakob, too long out of the center of attention, climbs into Peter's lap and straddles his wooden leg while the two grown men— one torn apart in the war and patched together again, the other too young to know anything but soft touches and kindness—size each other up.

85

"Husband," says Anna finally. "Goat-Cheese Willi's Klaus here has asked you a question."

"I heard him. I'm just wondering if he's done asking, or if there's something else on his mind."

"Well," says Klaus. "I suppose there is." He pauses and then yelps as Olga kicks him under the table, her impatience and excitement getting the upper hand.

"Olga and me would like to have the banns spoken," Klaus says, and with that he sets the rest of Olga's life in motion.

On the last night she will ever spend on her father's homestead, Barbara climbs the stairs to her narrow bed. Her things have been tied into bundles: clothes and linens, mostly. Tomorrow they will load all this on the wagon and the boys will set off to drive the sheep down the face of the Second Sister and across the village to River's Bend. She will come after; Alois will deliver her to her new home as he once delivered her as a bride to Half-Moon Hollow.

When she can find her way to sleep, Barbara drifts away measuring time. It is twenty-one years since Franz Michel died on the cobblestones; it is fifteen years since she first saw the Wainwright as a last chance for a home of her own and began taking her nighttime walks. It is ten years or more since anyone has spoken Franz Michel's name to her. In the haziness of half sleep, Barbara turns to the wall and begins to whisper that name, again and again, because she lives in fear of forgetting it as cleanly and absolutely as she has forgotten his beloved face.

Wainwright's Katharina

1938

When Wainwright's Katharina walked by, men paused and thought about turning around for a second look. Women took note of these thoughtful pauses; everybody talked. Katharina didn't much mind, even if her people did.

"It's from rolling up your skirt so high," said her half sister, Grumpy Marie.

"It's because she slinks like a cat in heat," corrected her father.

And Katharina would want to know what was so surprising about that: after all, an apple couldn't fall too far from the tree. Katharina would look directly at her mama when she said this, but if Theres didn't like being reminded that some in the village still thought of her as the Russian's whore, she kept it hid.

Katharina did work hard at getting the men to notice her, but it wasn't because she wanted a husband. When she looked at the available men in Rosenau, Wainwright's Katharina could see no promise in any of them but of children and farm work, things that interested her not in the least. If somebody bothered to ask, which nobody ever did, she could tell them what she had in mind: a life she had built for herself out of illustrated magazines. Somewhere in a city where the mountains did not crowd in, where there was sky. She saw herself as a shop clerk in a fancy apothecary with long, polished wooden counters and bright glass jars and a bell on the door that tinkled when people came in. Where they sold real cosmetics and perfume, scented soaps and facial creams. She would stand behind the counter with her hair cut short and wear a white linen coat with her name embroidered above the left breast: Marlene or Lilianne or Martine; about the name she could not quite make up her mind. But Katharina knew that there would be other people like her, people who cared about their clothes and their nails; people who knew nothing about, cared to know nothing about, the price of feed cake, who never gave cheese a thought except when they saw it on the table in front of them, who could not tell the difference between the stink of cowshit and the stink of pigshit.

Katharina's only concern was getting out. Which seemed pretty unlikely, until a textile concern from the Rhine Valley decided to put up a sock and stocking factory in Rosenau.

For sons with no claim on land who couldn't make a living from blacksmithing or carpentry alone, there would be work for cash; cash for things folks knew about but didn't count on much, things you couldn't buy in Rosenau. Radios. Fancy tractors. Milk coolers. Stoves that burned electricity instead of wood. Oranges. Rouge. People had plans, you could hear about them on the church square anytime a few men put their heads together. Dokwiese's Markus and Hannelore were talking about a bakery, with a plate glass window. People wanted to build a real schoolhouse now that they had a teacher of their own: Bent Elbow's Martha, come back home with a certificate, all the way from Innsbruck. Fellele's Hermann, who did most of the butchering for folks anyway, wanted to start up a proper shop, like the one his brother-in-law had down in Ackenau.

But the only thing about the new factory that interested Wainwright's Katharina was the truck that brought supplies every day and the men who drove the truck. For six years, since she was ten years old and the first motorcar had driven up the twisty-turny newly paved one-lane road from Ackenau to Rosenau just to show that it could be done, Katharina had had a ride in a motorcar on her mind.

The truck that serviced the building site was not, of course, an automobile, not strictly speaking. But Katharina was a realistic girl, and so she saw it as a start. The truck would not go down the road and disappear; it would go to a bigger village where there were other trucks, and cars and men who knew how to drive them, and then they would move on, and eventually there would be a city. Katharina wondered a little sometimes about what she might have to provide in return. Whatever it was, she would gladly pay. And if it meant lying down in the back seat of a black car with polished chrome headlights and running boards and letting somebody climb on top of her, she could live with that. That wasn't so much. For almost every morning of her whole life Katharina had heard her mother's day start in exactly that way, the creaking of the bed, the hoarse little whispers her father made, her mother's silence like a growing pile of stones. Her mother survived it, day after day, with an old man too full of piss and vinegar to act his eighty-six years; and for a lot less return, as far as Katharina could see.

Late that summer, Katharina started to worry. She had been flirting with many of the workers on the building site, but she hadn't yet found one willing to risk his job and let her climb into the cab of the truck for the ride down the mountainside, no matter how friendly she got, no matter how nicely she asked. Soon the factory would be finished, and soon enough the snow would start and the road would close until spring; the socks would pile up in the factory waiting for the thaw, but Katharina couldn't wait. From first snow to the spring seemed to Katharina longer than a lifetime, longer than she could bear.

On the last Tuesday in August, Katharina went down to the factory just before midday to see her latest: a flatlander with a strange northern-sounding name, who was in charge of running the telephone cable.

"*Schatz*," Jens called her, and "*Liebling*," as he pulled her into the shadows behind the factory. Katharina suspected that he talked so sweet not out of affection but because he had trouble remembering her name. But he was close to giving her what she wanted, so she let him press her up against the side of the factory. The freshly laid stucco prickled through her clothes as he kissed her. He made funny little noises and rubbed his hips against her and put his tongue in her mouth; Katharina made little noises back, very little ones: enough to keep him interested, not enough to be heard by the men working around the corner. When he slid his hand up under her skirt Katharina smiled.

"You driving down for more cable this afternoon?" she asked as he fumbled his way into her panties.

Later Katharina was glad she had stopped him when she did, because that afternoon the truck made its swing through the church square without pausing. She stood and watched it disappear down the mountainside; Jens was sitting on the flatbed, and he never even looked her way. But there was no time to waste on thoughts of revenge: already the green of the forests had begun to turn brittle, here and there a touch of scarlet or pale yellow. The sky was that distinct shade of deep blue that came with the fall.

She was contemplating the next most likely candidate when he walked into the shop. Another flatlander, this one named Rupert; at least a reasonable name. He wanted a tin of tobacco and maybe a kiss or two from Katharina; not that he came right out to say so, but she could see what he had on his mind. Katharina put on her brightest and best smile, the one she practiced in front of the mirror. For Rupert, the overseer, who made all the decisions on the building site and incidentally wore a wedding ring. Katharina was growing desperate.

Still, she found it hard to concentrate as he leaned his dirty elbows on the counter to talk to her. The truck would be up again on the afternoon run, and she watched for it, only half listening to him. Rupert was dreary: more of Hitler, more of politics. Wasn't anybody bored with this yet? she wanted to know. It had been five months, after all, and they had seen little of the Nazis. Who cared what they called the country, what difference did it make? Nobody was complaining about the sudden flow of money, she pointed out. And war, well, that was less than a rumor, more of a joke.

"We see enough of them out on the Rhine," he told her. "You don't want them up here too."

"How bad could they be?" she wondered.

He shrugged. "Bad enough. They shake things up."

"What things?" she asked absently, paging through a magazine until a pair of high-heeled shoes of deep blue with silver buckles claimed her attention.

"They got a way of showing up, moving things around. People, sometimes."

Katharina frowned. "What people?"

Rupert looked around the shop and out the window. He seemed uneasy, but Katharina waited. Men liked to preen themselves on what they knew, if a girl could just hold her tongue.

"Idiots, mostly."

With a sigh, Katharina turned back to her magazine.

"Just be glad you don't have to deal with them up here," Rupert said. "It's peaceful up here."

She snorted. "Peaceful as the grave, all right. And just as dead boring. What kind of cars do Nazis drive, anyway?"

Katharina wasn't expecting an immediate answer to her question, but it came around the corner not an hour later. A motorcar drove into the church square and stopped in front of the shop. It wasn't black but a deep glossy green with a cream-colored roof. The door opened, and out got Sister Gertrudis and Sister Hanspeter, who kept house for Father Ritter and had lately started up a home for old folks without kin.

Nuns in an emerald green Daimler, marveled Katharina. Some things were just beyond bearing.

She called to Grumpy Marie to take over the shop and went to claim her ride in the motorcar.

The driver was breathtaking. Katharina could hardly believe her luck, that someone young and good-looking and in uniform would be driving this car. She stood at the top of the stone steps and leaned over the rail to get a better look. Katharina barely knew where to spend her attention, on the car or the uniform. She had never seen the likes of either.

The soldier looked around the square, and Katharina could see him sizing up the village, considering the Golden Eagle. He wanted a beer, she figured. But if he went off to the Eagle he would be lost to her: Manuel would keep him pinned in a corner with his tired old stories of the Great War and a million questions, and Katharina would never get her chance.

So she leaned over the bannister, set her face in a friendly smile, and called to him in her best book German. "You must be thirsty," she said, and in a rush, "It's a hot day, have you come far?" Just to get his attention.

He turned his eyes on her, hazel, and he smiled; Katharina smiled back.

"This," the soldier said conversationally, "must be like living at the bottom of a bowl." He looked around at the Three Sisters leaning in over the village, at the sheer bulk of the Praying Hands. Katharina followed the movement of his eyes and saw with a start that there was a dusting of snow on Gunta Steeple.

"Yes," she said with some satisfaction. "It's just like that." Her mind was racing, trying to put together the words that would open the car door for her, when the soldier spoke again.

"I'm looking for Ignaz Metzler," he said to her in his strange inland Austrian. "I'm told he's called the Wainwright."

Katharina's plans were in shambles. The soldier was looking for her father, so there would be no sliding onto that leather seat and slipping away before anybody noticed. She had waited a long time for this opportunity, and while she went to get the old man she thought hard about how the situation might be saved.

The Wainwright was asleep on a stool in the smithy, snoring through the noise of Stante's hammering at a frozen wheel axle. Stante looked up from his work, sweat running down his face and glistening at the open neck of his shirt and on his muscular forearms. He grinned at Katharina, and although she was in a hurry and agitated, she took the time to smile back at him. Stante was old enough to be her father but simple enough to be her child, and Katharina trusted him. Many times he had provided comfort where no one else had noticed she needed any. And if he liked the look of her hips swaying in her skirts, so what? He had never touched her with anything but his eyes, and there was nothing but pure admiration in him.

Katharina shook her father awake and stepped back out of reach of his swatting arm; the Wainwright did not take lightly to having his naps disturbed. But he listened to her story and then followed her through the smithy and over the sill of the little swinging door that led into the house, down the cool dark hall into the shop, where she had left the soldier in Marie's care.

Normally Katharina had no interest in her father's business and could not be persuaded to stay around for talk of milk prices and hay crops. But now she leaned up against the door frame with her hands behind her and waited for her chance.

"You are Ignaz Metzler?" the soldier asked. "Known as the Wainwright?" His tone was easy but his eyes were not, and suddenly Katharina wondered what trouble her father might have got into.

"You have two grandsons called–" He hesitated, withdrew a piece of paper from his uniform blouse, and read. "Michel and Konstantin?"

When the Wainwright acknowledged all these things to be true, the soldier glanced at Marie busily ordering stacks of dry goods and Katharina standing guard at the door; Katharina widened her eyes at him. She took in his little jolt of recognition with satisfaction: he responded like any man to what she had to offer.

"Who are these women?" the soldier asked.

Katharina saw with a start that her father clearly wanted to spit in the soldier's face, but was afraid to. There wasn't much the Wainwright shied away from; he would smack other people's children when they got within reach, and spit tobacco juice on the floor of the church just when it was quiet enough for everybody to hear him. He did what he wanted, and if somebody had something to say he would grin his toothless, unsettling grin and announce that he was senile and what did they want to do about that? But he was holding back now, and that made Katharina nervous all over again.

"These are my daughters," the Wainwright said finally, his voice crackling. He spoke dialect and let the soldier fend for himself.

But the soldier had understood. He looked from Katharina to Marie and could hardly hide his surprise and distrust. Marie was a woman close to sixty, the second child of her father's first marriage; dumpy and gray, she squinted at the world because she was too vain to wear spectacles. *I'll never look like that,* Katharina wanted to say to the soldier. *I'd hang myself first.*

"Half sisters," she said instead. "We're half sisters. Forty-two years old she was when I was born."

The soldier was eyeing Marie closely. "Are you the mother of Konstantin and Michel?" he asked. When she denied this, he cut off her long story of a dead brother and sister-in-law and the twins' birth, and turned back to the Wainwright.

"I have a report that your grandsons are feeble."

The Wainwright raised an eyebrow in surprise. "Well, goddamn," he said lightly.

95

"This is official business," the soldier said. "A report has been filed. I'm here to verify it."

Grinning, the Wainwright turned to Katharina. "Take this flatlander and show him how feeble your nephew Stante is," he said.

Katharina could have kissed her father in gratitude; instead she inclined her head toward the soldier and gestured for him to follow her to the smithy. He had to duck at every doorway, and Katharina stopped to watch him, playing for time, thinking how strange it was to have him walking through this house, built for smaller men. She noted how the floor creaked under his weight, how shiny his hair was. She wondered if he noticed the smell of frying onions and milk set to sour.

Her mother came to the kitchen door and looked at the soldier; her face twitched slightly at the sight of his uniform. For one strange moment Katharina had the idea that her mother was actually going to say something to this soldier when she hadn't spoken five words to anyone in the last year. But then

Theres stepped back into the kitchen with one hand over her heart, her pale face a streak in the dim light.

Katharina tried to smile at him over her shoulder. "What kind of accent is that you've got?" she asked. "I don't recognize it."

He looked surprised. "Vienna. You've never heard a Viennese talk? Not even on the radio?"

"We don't have a radio," said Katharina. "I've never seen a Viennese before." She paused. "Did you give the nuns a ride up from Ackenau?" she asked. "Or from farther?"

"From Ackenau."

"Do you give anybody a ride who asks you?"

"That depends," he said.

Satisfied, Katharina led him into the smithy.

Stante was still at the anvil, hammering with a speed that seemed at odds with his easy swings. The metal shouted out and roared. Under his leather apron his shirt was stained in concentric circles of sweat. He looked tremendously fit and able.

"He's the second-strongest man in the village," Katharina said. "The only one who can best him is Hickar's Tonile's Dokus."

"Tell him I want to talk to him." The soldier was not impressed.

Katharina shrugged and waved at Stante to get his attention. With a great grin, he put down his hammer and came over to talk, wiping his forehead on his shirt sleeve. When he realized the man was a stranger, Stante's usual open expression faded just a bit.

"You are Metzler, Konstantin, year of birth 1901?" the soldier asked, and when Stante nodded: "You have a twin brother named Michel?"

Stante nodded again and wet his lips with his tongue, a quick swipe, but it made Katharina wince; it was the only habit that gave him away.

"Where is your brother?"

"He's down at River's Bend," Katharina answered for Stante. "Michel don't get out much."

"I'm talking to him," the soldier said.

Katharina raised an eyebrow. "Well, maybe he's shy. Maybe it will take a little time for him to get up the courage to talk to you. You scare some folks more than others," she added, hoping she could tease him out of this serious tone.

"Can you read and write?" the soldier asked Stante.

Stante's smile had faded away completely. He looked uncertainly between Katharina and the soldier.

"Can you do sums? Do you have fits?" Then, with a sideways glance at Katharina: "Do you have sexual relations with normal women?"

"Hey!" Katharina drew herself up. "What kind of questions are those?" She felt the heat of the forge suddenly, sweat on her own forehead and at the collar of her dress.

Ignoring her, the soldier started his list of questions again. Katharina inserted herself between him and Stante. "No, no, no, and no," she shouted.

The soldier turned and walked away.

In the shop, the Wainwright was hunched over the candy jar, fishing with two gnarled fingers for a peppermint at the bottom. When the soldier came back with Katharina close behind he looked up, showing his bare gums and a mouthful of hard candy.

"I have orders to take your grandsons with me to the evaluation station in Hohenems," the soldier said. "I'll take them now."

Marie drew in a sharp breath.

"Can he do that?" Katharina asked her half sister, her father.

"I'll take them now," he repeated.

"Let me see those orders," Grumpy Marie said in her best postmistress voice. When she had read the papers, she nodded at her father.

"When will they come back?" the Wainwright asked.

"When they've been evaluated."

"How long will that be? I can't do without Stante. Repairs piling up."

The soldier shrugged. "As long as it takes. A few days. A week. Where is the twin?"

"Down to the River's Bend homestead. A woman looks after him, Bengat's Barbara." A thought chased across the Wainwright's face; it was not unpleasant to him, that was clear, although he tried to hide it. "You'll have to go through her to get to Michel."

"You are the legal guardian?" the soldier asked.

The Wainwright nodded.

The soldier put a paper down in front of him and pointed to a spot at the bottom. "Sign here, and tell me where this River's Bend is."

In a rambling and hesitant manner, Marie began to give directions to the homestead.

"He can't go that way," the Wainwright said impatiently. "The car won't manage that cow path. He'll have to go down the other side of the stream and circle around in the field next to the house and come back up, loop through the square again."

The soldier turned to Katharina. "You will show me the way to River's Bend," he said. Seeing her confusion and mistaking it for unwillingness, he added, "It's just a motorcar. Nothing will happen to you in it."

The seats were leather, leather so fine and soft that her fingertips left little moons behind. The dashboard was rosewood, polished to a high gloss. Fixed to it was a small crystal vase in a silver ring that caught the sunlight and scattered it. A single wilted white rose hung its blowsy head from the vase, giving off the last of its scent.

Stante was fond of flowers, and Katharina tried to point the rose out to him, but he seemed not to hear. In the few minutes they had been allowed, Marie had thrown some clothes, soap, and a razor into an old cardboard suitcase. Now Stante clasped this to his chest and stared at the back of the soldier's head. Katharina tried to take in all the details of the car, but Stante was distracting. Finally she took his hand, hard as a board and rougher, and cradled it in her own. They drove through the village and down the river's edge, the car pitching over the rutted path. Katharina saw Bent Elbow's Johanna on horseback and waved, but Johanna just stopped right there with her mouth gaping wide and didn't think to wave back. The car came to a stop when the path did, and the soldier asked if this was the homestead called River's Bend.

Katharina was afraid he would want her to come in with him to explain to Michel and Barbara, but he got out of the car without a word and went through the *Schopf* into the house. Katharina sat silently holding Stante's hand, listening to the tick of the cooling motor. His hand was very cold, she thought, and her own hand sweaty.

"There's nothing to worry about," she said, mostly to herself. "It's just an evaluation." But Stante didn't raise his head or answer her.

"You'll be home soon," she went on.

Then the door opened and let out the sound of wailing. Barbara was following on the soldier's footsteps as he came out of the house, crying as she stumbled along. The soldier carried Michel in his arms. Katharina saw this, Michel's long twisted legs over the soldier's arm, and she felt her stomach turn over and begin to churn. She wished she could get out of the car and just run away, but Stante's hand clenched hers more tightly and he groaned, as if he somehow knew she was thinking of leaving him alone.

Barbara was wringing her hands in her apron and talking to the soldier in a loud voice. The soldier kicked at the car door. Awkwardly, her fingers fumbling at the latch, Katharina opened it. The sound of Barbara's crying intensified. In a single quick motion the soldier dumped Michel onto the seat on Katharina's other side.

Stante refused to look at his brother; he covered his head with his arms and curled forward, his forehead on his knees.

Barbara came to the closed window and held her face up against the glass. In one hand she clutched the paper the Wainwright had signed. Katharina leaned over Michel to open the window. Barbara reached through to stroke his misshapen head, trying to soothe his tears though her own were choking her.

"Where are you taking them?" she wailed again and again. "When are they coming back? Can't I come along? They're scared, can't you see they're scared? Katharina, Katharina, tell him. Tell him."

The soldier started the car without answering her, and Barbara chased around to the other side and put her face to his window. "Just down to Ackenau?" she shrilled. "Until they've calmed a little!"

This made him pause.

"I'll walk back!" Barbara said breathlessly. "I can walk back."

Katharina looked at Barbara and saw what he must be seeing: an old woman in a stained dark blue apron, iron gray braids around her head, a thin pale mouth, the veins on her soft cheeks like webs spun of fine scarlet silk, magnified by tears.

"No," he said after seeming to consider for a moment. "But I'll let the girl come along, down to Ackenau. To keep them calm." He twisted in the driver's seat to look at Katharina. "She can walk back." Katharina's puzzled look seemed to amuse him. "If you would like a ride, that is. *Schatz.*"

The car moved back over the rutted path. Word had spread and now there were people, some of them curious, others angry. Bengato Jakob leaped across the stream and came rushing up toward the car but then fell quickly out of sight; Katharina thought he must have tripped. The car was creeping along, and folks had time to bend down and look in the windows, to mouth words at her. They crowded up close, pointing at the driver, fingering the standard with its embroidered swastika. Calling questions out, to her, to each other. Hands flitting against the window glass, calloused red palms. For a good ways Barbara walked behind, crying loudly, calling, "Be good, boys, be good, come back soon. I'm waiting for you."

Michel was clutching at Katharina, his bent hands twisting in her skirt. Katharina put an arm around him. She hadn't seen Michel in a long time; he never came into the village, and she couldn't remember the last time she had been out at River's Bend. His blond hair was thin at the crown. He hiccuped, and then was silent.

She tried to take Stante's hand again, but he turned away from her to watch the village slip by. The car looped through the church square. Marie stood silent in the shop door, waving a handkerchief. The Wainwright was nowhere in sight. No sign of her mother. Suddenly she wanted some sight of her mother. The car turned onto the paved road, and Katharina caught movement from the corner of her eye; a woman was running full out behind them, her feet drumming, her apron fluttering. Katharina looked at Stante: his gaze was fixed ahead, he didn't see his Aunt Anna racing after them. Then the car sped up and Anna fell back and disappeared.

There was a view as they made their way down toward Ackenau, but Katharina turned around, twisting this way and that as the car took the curves, first to the right, then to the left, her neck bent to look back and up the mountainside. Rosenau appeared and disappeared, came and went. Michel had fallen asleep with his head on her shoulder; his spit dribbled onto her dress. Like a baby, Katharina thought. A thirty-seven-year-old baby.

A glint of red caught her eye, there under Michel's foot, and she leaned forward to pull at it: a hair ribbon. Katharina stared at it, a worn satin ribbon tied into a bow, a strand of dark hair caught in the knot. A ribbon such as a child would wear. Dizzy, she drew in breath and the smells of leather and wood polish and roses, and now she noticed, buried not too far under those fine smells, the stink of urine, the sweet smell of vomit.

The soldier was talking to her.

"How far do you want to go?" he was asking Katharina. "Is Ackenau far enough? Just how far do you want to go?"

Mikatrin

Bent Elbow Homestead 1943

Aunt Johanna has got it into her head that Blossom has to stay. No matter what I have to say about it, Hanna has that cow in her head and she won't turn her loose.

I want to get to bed. Not that the work's done, you understand: even with the farm scaled way back, I can't keep up. But I've been on my feet since before sunrise, and I don't much want to argue about that cow.

Hanna looks at me with her watery eyes, eyes such a pale blue that I imagine the color washed away over the years by the tears always pooling, ready to fall.

"That's a good cow," she tells me. "A fine animal."

There's a lump of cream at the bottom of my glass, pale yellow. This is the color the cream takes on when the cows are first put out to pasture, where wildflowers make good fodder in the spring: celandine and avens, lady's mantle and cowslip.

"We can't afford Blossom," I say. "We don't need two cows, just the two of us."

"It won't be just the two of us forever," she shoots right back. "You got a sister, if you'd care to remember. A family." She pokes up her chin, daring me to contradict her.

I feel the anger crawling over my chest, up my neck.

"We can't keep a cow who is only interested in raiding the garden and gives us nothing in return."

"Then you'll be calling the butcher for me next!" Spittle flies from the corner of her mouth; color rises on her papery cheeks. There's no denying how Johanna has aged since this war began. She is sixty-four years old, but she shows every day of it, every minute, and more. I see there's no arguing with her tonight, and I'm about to give in when from out back there's a long bellow.

My chair totters and threatens to fall, I'm in such a hurry to be out the door. Hanna is right behind me, her cane thumping away.

The stag is standing where he always does when he comes to call, on the crest just above the homestead where the forest gives way to Hutla Meadow and then the upper pastures. His rack must be close to two meters across; his white chest is a jagged star in the forest. He bellows again, and the sound echoes and rolls over the mountain.

"Ain't he a sight," Hanna whispers, as if he might hear her and bolt.

"It's time to go to bed," I answer her, turning away. The meanness in my voice shames me. Lately it seems during the day I have my hands full trying to keep it in check. At night, when I'm tired, it pours out of me like blood.

In the morning, after I finish milking the two cows we have left, or should I say after I milk Bessie and try to milk Blossom, I muck out the stalls and feed the pig and the chickens and put the cows and the horse out to the homestead pasture, and then I head into the house for breakfast. I've got half an hour to eat, clean myself up, and get to work in the village.

Aunt Johanna has fixed a breakfast of boiled eggs, mountain cheese, and tea made with leaves used twice before, so thin with milk it's lost all personality. She sits at the table with a newspaper right up to her face; sometimes she has a smudge of ink on the end of her nose all day.

"It says here the war's going real well," Hanna tells me. She tells me this every day: the paper is more than two weeks old, but she keeps reading it out loud to me.

"That cow will not let down her milk," I respond. "She just will not. She don't give me half the amount I get from Bessie."

Hanna holds up her fingers, chapped red and knotty with the arthritis, and clutches at the air as if she were milking. "You don't sweet-talk her," she tells me for the hundredth time. "It's all in the talk." She looks at me wide-eyed, unflinching: my mother's eyes, but not my mother. That used to confuse me; now it just makes me mad.

"I'll stop in and have a word with Hermann today," I tell her as I head into the bedroom to wash the smell of the cowshed off of me and change for work. "He'll think my talk is sweet enough, all right. I'll send him out today."

Her voice rises and breaks as it tries to follow me behind closed doors. "I'll send him on his way if he shows his face here, I certainly will!" Then: "I will not let that animal go to meat! Do you hear? You'll not send your sister's cow to the butcher because you're too ornery to get milk out of her!"

I look at my face in the mirror, and my own blue eyes start to swim. I see my mother's face, but not my mother. I see a woman almost thirty years old who looks closer to forty. I see a woman who used to be a daughter, a wife, a mother, but now is none of those things. I see a woman drying out and down to bitterness and bone.

The factory is an unhealthy pink color like fish gone bad; its thick walls are always clammy to the touch. When I complain about this, the other women tell me that at least it's cool inside, and I tell them that's exactly the problem: it's being inside in the summer when there's work waiting in the fields.

When I pull up on my bike, Wainwright's Katharina and Fellele's Marianne are leaning against that fleshy pink with their upper bodies, heads thrown back, their heels in the ground as if to hold that wall just where it stands and keep it from walking away. They are sharing a bar of chocolate, eating the last of it before the late bell rings. They suck the stickiness from their fingers noisily.

"Never seen chocolate?" Katharina asks me when I catch her eye. She is daring me to wonder who she got it from, and how.

"Not in a few years, I haven't," I answer her as I walk on past.

They find this amusing, or at least they find me amusing. Their laughter follows me until I am up the stairs and past Dokwiese's Harald, who clocks me in with a mumbled *Heil Hitler* and a little click of the tongue to let me know how close I have come to losing an hour's pay. I pass long lines of sewing machines where other women are getting down to work, and finally I walk into the room where I will spend the day feeding and unknotting and retying an endless skein of thread into a machine that will never have enough, because it will never be done weaving gauze, because there will never be enough bandages, because this war will never end.

Through the window, dusty with the gray fluff I cough up

in the night, I see that Wiar's Markus has put their milch cows out to pasture; one of them lifts a rear leg and shakes the hoof repeatedly as if she's got some trouble there.

They let us go at four, those of us who have livestock or other concerns at home and no men to look after things: I set off with Kolobano Kaspar's Elisabeth, Barbara from the Hill, and Olga from the church square dairy, who was once my sister-in-law but now is just another woman whose husband is in the Ukraine somewhere and whose brothers have all fallen and whose mother wanders the village at night calling for them in a uneasy whisper.

Olga is gone before I can catch her attention. I wanted to ask her about Blossom, get her opinion, but I suppose it's no good to let Harald see us talking outside the factory. He might try to add some hours to our workday.

The bike rattles and hitches on the last stretch, the little hill up to the house. I am thinking about that—about where I will get the grease for the chain—when I come around the corner and there is Blossom.

She stands in the middle of the garden, hooves spread out at angles in the dark loose earth of the carrot beds, while she eats not from the turnip or potato tops or from the tender new shoots of cabbage or from the leaves on the tomato plants, but from my one small bed of flowers, tearing out ragged clumps of petunias and geraniums, pansies and daisies barely big enough to get between her teeth.

This is when I remember that I forgot to call in at the butcher's on the way home.

I'm ready to jump right back on that bike and do the job, get Hermann out here now to cart Blossom away, her stomachs full of the best and sweetest of my garden. Bessie can wait another half hour, I think to myself as I pick up the rug beater that hangs on the wall under the laundry line and start in on Blossom.

She is not greatly bothered: she looks around curiously, as if to ask me what it is I think I am accomplishing, and then ambles out of the garden. I beat her all the way back to the cowshed. I work myself into a sweat. I beat her until my arm is sore, and then I put my head down on her flank, warm and dusty and smelling sweet, the high, keen sweetness of milk and manure and piss, and I let the tears come. It seems now, at this moment, that I will never be able to move again.

When I do move, it's not to pick up my bike and head for town, or to get Bessie into the cowshed and milk her, or to start cleaning up the garden. I move because I hear Aunt Johanna laughing, a sixteen-year-old giggle from a woman more than sixty years old, a giggle that means that she is not alone.

He looks up, still laughing, when I come into the kitchen. My braids fly loose around my head, my face is burning hot. His own face sobers a little bit, and this is what gets Johanna's attention. She turns around in her chair, one arm hooked over the back. Her eyes flash; this man has stolen twenty good years off her face just by walking into her kitchen and sitting down. She motions to me.

"Come on in and say hello," she says. "Say hello to the Cobbler's Youngest."

That's what people always called him, the Cobbler's Youngest. When he went to school with my younger sister he answered to it just as he did to his own name.

"Martin has brung us some good news from the East," Hanna offers.

She has made him coffee, the very last of our coffee, a smell that fills this kitchen with ghosts: my mother with her hands wrapped around her cup for the warmth, my father sloshing brown sugar into his in sloppy spoonfuls. "The smell of your coffee would wake the dead," he says to Mama now. She laughs in response; I hear her.

"From your sister," Martin says. The voice is familiar, but the man is a stranger. He looks at me with his sunburned face and high forehead and over-blue eyes, and he is no man I've ever known. He reaches up from his seat to shake my hand; his palm is hard and his fingers are calloused. A working man's hand.

Now I see what's on the table between them: a letter in a dirty gray envelope. My name is on it in my sister's handwriting, small and cramped, the black ink twisting on the paper like snakes.

"When did you get in?" I ask him, turning away.

"Yesterday."

"You working for the mail service instead of for the artillery these days? Or are you just home for a holiday?"

Silence follows me across the room to the sink; it stays a while as I wash my face and hands.

When I turn back to them, my face still hot but clean, I see the crutch propped up in the corner. Under the table there are three feet, and two of them are Aunt Johanna's.

"The cows are waiting," I tell him, looking him straight in the eye. "I've got to tend to the milking." And I get out to the barn, fast, before it's his turn to ask questions that I don't want to think about, let alone answer.

On the way out I say to no one in particular, "You left the garden gate open again."

I leave them there, the mute letter on the table between them.

The barn door swings open just as I finish with Bessie and sit down to milk Blossom. She is not one bit distracted by Martin: she knows I'm coming at her with the bucket. Blossom swings her horns at me in a lazy circle as far as she can go, tethered like she is. She would surely do more if she could. She takes this bucket personal, whereas the rug beater, that was only mildly irritating.

"Goddamn cow," I croon softly. "Old bitch. No-good god-forsaken shitty-assed nag."

The bucket is barely down under her before she kicks it away with a little tap.

I am about to start the tiresome business of tying a rope to a fetlock so I can winch it up—on three legs even Blossom can only dream about kicking—when Martin hitches on over, swinging his peg, negotiating with the crutch. He stops behind Blossom, and then he grabs her tail and twists hard, yanking it up high.

Blossom lets out a terrific bellow, mad as hell. She forgets what I want from her. It's enough to let me get started.

"That is a cantankerous female," Martin says when she takes a breath.

The top of my head is pressed into Blossom's side. I can't see much of him except his trouser leg and the peg underneath it.

"A-yo. Nothing but cantankerous females around this place."

The stream ebbs: she has given me three liters when Bessie gave me nine.

"You stingy bitch," I tell Blossom. "Who are you saving your precious milk for?"

"Her calf," suggests Martin.

And because I know he is right, because I know this foolish animal is waiting for a calf long gone to meat, I get madder, which makes me careless. I move too quick when I reach for the bucket, jostling her udder, and in response Blossom flicks out again neatly: the milk pours out over the ground.

"Hanna says I don't sweet-talk her enough," I tell Martin as we watch the milk spread through the straw and mingle with the yellow stream in the dunging channel. "It's a talent I don't possess."

"Well, I suppose it don't matter much," Martin says. "Given the line you married into. Our daddy always said that the Bengat boys had an uncommon hand for a reluctant animal."

I seek out his face to make sure what I hear in his voice is real. He doesn't know.

"Leo fell last year. In Norway."

His eyes flicker; I have surprised him. "I just mentioned Leo's name to Johanna, and she didn't say a word. She brightened right up."

I don't know why I should blush, but there it is. "I expect she did. She was fond of him, and the facts haven't caught her up yet." I busy myself with cleaning up the mess under Blossom. She watches me, shifting on her hind legs, but I suppose she is satisfied with the evening's work; she leaves me be and gets on with her cud.

Now Martin tells me something I already know. "Leo was a good man," he says.

Sympathy still don't sit well on my stomach, but this is the truth, and I must acknowledge it. I have come that far since Leo fell. I nod.

Martin shakes his head, as if to push away an unwelcome thought. "That means all of the Bengat homestead boys except Jakob are gone."

"Jakob fell, they got word just a few weeks ago."

Martin leans against the wall. "The farm?"

"Anna let out the fields, sold the animals."

"The Bengat dairy?"

"Closed up. We take our milk to Olga and her boys, now that they've started dairying full time. When there's enough to bother. Anna's there with them too, for the time being. She's taken it all pretty hard."

He clears his throat. When he looks at me, his eyes are swimming but his mouth is set. He clears his throat again; something about this, the way he shifts his leg and straightens, makes me tense up.

"The letter is addressed to you," Martin says.

When I don't answer, he continues anyway.

"She'll be home real soon," he says.

My curiosity gets the best of me, and I let him get on with this story that he's fixed on telling me.

An expression comes over Martin's face, half hard, half confused. He looks like a man who has given up on good luck but has found some, sudden. And maybe it's luck he hasn't earned, but he's going to take it where he finds it.

"I ran into Martha in the village where the hospital is. Where they took my leg off." His gaze is focused somewhere else, far away.

"It was about three months ago now, and the snow was still on the ground, but when they finally let me step out–" He glances down at the peg where it rests in the muck. "The first morning they let me loose, I was still sore as hell from this thing, and not in the best of moods, I have to admit. And I step outside and I'm standing there in the cold and my leg seizes up and I think I'm going to fall flat on my face, and then I look up and there's Martha standing in front of me. Trailing a whole shabby band of village kids, on her way to teach school."

Martin's chin is down on his chest, but he manages to look at me, asking me to ask him to go on with this.

I keep hold of his gaze, I won't let it go.

"And she smiles at me, just as simple as that, and she says, 'Cobbler's Youngest, you are going to catch an awful chill.'"

His eyes are on me.

"They're going to reassign her to a local school, maybe right here in the village."

A ball of acid shoots up from my belly into my throat and I have to spit it out.

"Not damn likely," I say. "They sent in a man from Vienna, he's made himself comfortable here."

"But it's her home," he says, again telling me something I know already. "It's her hometown."

I wipe my face on my sleeve, and I have to wonder a little at how dull a man can be sometimes. It seems this particular man left his leg behind him but didn't learn anything about the war in the process.

"They sent her away, didn't they?" I tell him. "Sent her almost all the way to the Front. The Sudetenland is her home now."

"She's Austrian," Martin says, pulling up stiff.

"There is no Austria anymore," I remind him. "No Czechoslovakia, for that matter. And didn't your daddy vote for Vorarlberg to break away from the Empire back in '19?"

Martin almost lets me change the subject, he almost rises to this bait, but then he gets a hold of his temper. After a while he says, not really to me, "She never told me."

My laugh is a sorry thing, a kind of bark, rough and short and more than a bit of a threat. "They sent her there as a punishment because she walked out of the meeting for the grade school teachers right before the loyalty oath."

He opens his mouth, but I cut him off quick. I cut him off because I know what he is going to say, about how brave Martha was to stand up to the damn Germans when most folks just gave right in, and some with a smile and a wink. It is something I have heard too many times. So I cut him off and I step toward him with what I have to say plain on my face.

"Martha said her piece and didn't look back when she had to leave me here with an old woman and a baby and the farm and not enough cash to last three months," I shoot at him.

"Most all the animals had to go to meat–and believe me the army took more than their fair share. I barely get enough hay in to feed these few sorry creatures over the winter. I spend my days down at the factory trying to earn enough cash to keep things going. Martha stood up to those Germans, yes she did, but she left me with this cow," I say, slapping Blossom's bony back. "She took a liking to this cow when it was calved, and hand-fed it and ruined it, and now Hanna won't let me sell her. Because what Martha wants, Martha gets." Usually, I add to myself. But maybe not this time.

When I catch my raggedy breath and calm myself down, I see he is not afraid of me, not even put off by the anger that streams out of me. He meets me eye for eye, straight on. He is curious. My skin rises in bumps at this, because now I know what I have only suspected, way down deep, in the place where a woman's suspicions are born and where they fester: this man and I will be conducting business together.

I pick up the bucket of milk I got from Bessie and I turn to leave, but he stops me.

"Where is your little girl, where's Maria?"

"Maria's dead," I tell him, and I head for the pig, because the pig hasn't been fed, and pigs can't wait.

I get up, I do what I have to do in the cowshed, I eat, I go to work. On the way home I cycle right past the butcher's empty shopwindow. What are you feeling guilty about, I ask myself, pedaling faster.

Why are you in a hurry?

I come down the valley and start uphill. As a girl I could pedal this bike all the way, take every curve without breathing hard. But lately I have begun walking the bike once I pass the Tanna Hanso homestead, until I come around Bent Elbow curve.

Once I see the homestead, I breathe easier. It sounds crazy, I know, but sometimes when I stand in front of that machine all day I get this idea that the farm will just up and disappear without me there, that I'll come around this corner and there will be nothing, no homestead, just unclaimed land wild with wood sorrel and bitter crab, nettles and pigweed, the bone white cliffs of the Praying Hands rising naked and treeless behind it all.

Martin's there in the garden.

I stand for a minute watching him. It's a little awkward, the way he swings the shovel while trying to keep his balance, but he's doing a decent job. The flower beds have been cleaned up, and they are ready for planting. Next to Martin is a box of seedlings. He looks at me and then looks back at his hands, covered with dirt.

"I brought them from home," he says. "From my sister's garden. I don't know that they'll take to being transplanted."

"Work to do in the barn," I mumble. I need to get away from him, right now, before I say things I will regret. Before I get down there in the dirt with him and take his face in my hands and ask him to tell me about Martha.

But in the barn there is nothing for me to do: he's mucked out the pens, brushed Claudius down. He's even got a decent amount of milk out of Blossom. She turns to look at me now: there's no mistaking a disgruntled cow. She had not counted on Martin.

In the kitchen, Aunt Johanna is busy putting dinner on the table. She's gone to some trouble, and her color is up, two red flags flying high.

"What's he doing here?" I ask her straight out.

"Why, we need a man around here and he needs work," she says, putting soup bowls on the table.

I wait. It's my one real advantage with Hanna: I can usually wait her out. After a while she begins to squirm and send nervous, sidelong looks my way. Then she says, "You need the help."

"What'll we pay him?" I ask evenly.

"Room and board."

"He's got a bed and a home of his own. He's got a homestead of his own, too."

"Two older brothers don't leave him much over," Hanna points out.

"That's his misfortune and none of mine. I don't need him." I fight with the panic that rises up.

She rounds on me. "Don't be a fool," she hisses. "You do need this man. The farm needs him."

"But Martha wants him," I say, and the visible shock this gives her leaves me with a sour-sweet satisfaction.

She tries to gather her thoughts, I can see her struggling.

When Martin comes into the kitchen five minutes later,
we are still facing off across the table, the two of us, at a draw.

There is no moon tonight. It is so dark that I can't see my hand in front of my face. As dark as on the inside of a cow, Hanna would say if she were here with me. But she's in the house, asleep.

I stand here alone, my back against the wall of the barn, listening. The cows are at rest, drawing in air with a deep hum, letting it go with a rush. I can hear the straw stirring around them in uneasy whirpools. I can hear the sow's nails scrabbling as she searches for a more comfortable position. I can hear Martin, his heartbeat.

When the stag stays away, I climb the stairs to the hayloft, feeling my way as I go. I let my nose lead me to him. He is an island of sweat rising out of a scant sea of hay, built of blood and bone. When I have found him, he reaches up to take my hand and pulls me down onto the blanket.

"How did you milk that cow?" I ask him.

"I know a little bit about sweet-talking," he says to me. "It's one of my few talents."

His cheeks are rough. His mouth tastes of barley soup and the new strawberries we had for supper. His hands in my hair, on my shoulders, on the small of my back, under my hips.

When we are done with each other, it don't take long, he starts to speak. I put my hand over his mouth.

"Last summer when we went up to mow Hutla Meadow, Maria got bored playing on the wagon. She fussed at me until I let her go ahead of us home. She drowned in the well. We found her when we got back."

I don't tell him the rest. I don't tell him how after that day Johanna's face was struck to sudden stone and her normal steady stream of commentary just dried up. When she came around, months later, she couldn't always remember who was living and who wasn't.

Most of all, I don't tell Martin about Maria. I don't describe to him the face of a four-year-old child when she's been upside down in water, the face I dream every night is at my breast with milky eyes rolling freely, untethered like a newborn's, her swollen blue cheeks working, working, working, trying to suckle the life out of me.

Martin is so quiet I might as well be alone here in the dark if it weren't for the salty smell, the stickiness between us.

What is there to say, after all?

Then he searches out my hand and puts it on the bare stump of his leg. I feel the pulsing of the veins close to the surface, the raised scars winding under my fingertips. Instead of a knee there are neat tucks and folds of muscle and skin, firm and soft all at once.

I wonder now if he screamed. I wonder if he has nightmares.

"I had been thinking about marrying Martha when she comes home," Martin says, his voice hoarse. He thinks he is telling me something I don't already know.

I let my hand travel up the stump of his leg until I find

what is left of him. This time, it takes longer. There's a taste in my mouth, a taste I had almost forgotten: the coppery taste of getting what I need, of getting enough.

Saturday. A fine sunny late spring day, and Hutla Meadow is overripe for mowing. I have been putting it off.

Martin practices with the scythe for a while out behind the barn; he tries to balance himself without his crutch while he swings the blade. I'm afraid he'll take his other leg off, but I know better than to watch him; I force myself to go hitch Claudius to the wagon, sharpen the other blade, load the rakes and forks.

Hanna comes out with a jug of water and lunch tied up in an old towel: buttered bread, cheese, some dried meat. I raise an eyebrow when I see how she has raided our cellar. She stares right back at me.

"Men in the field need their food," she says. Then she heads back for the house, leaning heavily on her cane, her skirts trailing in the dirt.

"Where you going?" I call after her.

She turns back. Rarely have I seen such a look of disgust on her face.

I am overcome with shame; I am flushed with defiance.

Hanna stomps back to the wagon and shields her eyes to look up to where I stand on the flatbed.

"I'm a grown woman," I remind her before she can start in on me. "I know my own mind. I had a husband, but I don't anymore. I have borne a child."

"What does that have to do with it?" she says, taken aback.

Then, because I am not as free of guilt as I want her to think I am, because she is my mother's sister, because I am my mother's daughter, I say, "Please, Auntie. Please."

"You don't want me at Hutla Meadow today," she sniffs.

"Of course I want you."

Hanna looks to make sure that Martin is out of earshot, then she reaches up and pokes me in the ribs with her cane, hard.

"You don't want me at that meadow today, Mikatrin. Not if you have a copper's worth of sense in your head, not if you know what you need."

"I need him," I say, these words slippery on my tongue, sliding away before I can reach out and grab them.

And they seem to wash all the irritation out of her. The crease between her brow smooths, and her face unfolds into something that is half pain, half understanding. Johanna looks away from me and over the farm she has worked most of her adult life. I see words working at her, trying to come up from someplace she has kept them tied down, but she fails. She fails to give me permission to do what I must do, but she does not forbid me, either.

"Of course you do," she says, and then she turns on her heel to retreat to the house, where she closes the door quietly behind herself.

Daddy inherited the farm from his father, who bought it when it was just a *Vorschaß*. Grandpa Jos put in the garden, bought two milch cows, and started haying. He died of a fever and passed the land on to his only son, my father, who was made of the same kind of muscle and sweat. Daddy saved enough to buy Hutla Meadow in '36. Back then it was Austria. When he died–cutting this very grass, with his scythe in mid swing–it wasn't Austria anymore. But it don't seem to make much difference what it's called. The weather is fine, or it rains. The animals live and thrive, or we send them to the butcher.

Johanna never got along with Hans, but even she will admit it. The Bent Elbow homestead is something to be proud of: it may be steep and hard to get to, but it's all clover and timothy. Good meadowland, healthy animals.

Daddy passed it all on to Leo and me.

It is a strong urge in me to point out to Martin that the homestead, the pastures and meadows, the *Vorschaß* at Gunta Steeple that we can't quite see from here, because it is hidden from our view by the ridges of the Second Sister, the livestock, the wooden handles of these scythes that soak up our sweat, belong to me, and to me alone. If I should fall under the wheels of the wagon, or if a hayfork should come spinning out of the loft and pin me down, or if some hidden place in my head should start to bleed and I should die today, the farm would go to Martha. I have no children to pass it all on to.

Martin is working on the other side of the parcel, moving up the incline while I move down. He is making steady progress, but he is slow. The strip he leaves behind him is uneven, as if he were a boy cutting for the first time, not a man who has done this all his life.

When we finish, he has mowed about half the amount I have, and I see on his face that this does not sit well with him. Maybe a cobbler's bench would suit him better, I think, but I fight hard to swallow this back down and not say it out loud.

We sit down under a tree to eat our lunch, and his color evens out.

"I'll be back in the rhythm soon," he says when he is full, pushing his hair back out of his face. Then he lies down in the shade of the tree and pulls his hat over his eyes.

I turn on one side and put my hand on his shirtfront to follow its rise and fall. He lifts one arm and pulls my head down to his chest. The rolling beat of his heart makes my own heart beat easier.

Late afternoon we have turned the grass so that it will dry even. Tomorrow, unless it rains in the night, we'll come up again to load the wagon with new hay and haul it back to the barn.

Martin is pale and his hair is slick with sweat. When he throws the hayfork in the wagon, his hands are trembling. There is a dark red patch where the cut-off pant leg meets the peg. Not that I point this out: I have more sense than that.

We are perched on the seat, bracing ourselves with feet and hands against the incline. To our right, I can just see it through the trees, is the spring that feeds our well. When I was a girl, I spent every free minute in that wood; I don't expect I'll ever go back again.

We are on our way back to the homestead. On our way home.

Claudius takes the turn out of the forest, and everything is spread out below us: to the south the Three Sisters and the rest of the mountains down the valley ranging up behind them; bedded at the foot of the Second Sister, the village; to the west, eventually, the Rhine Valley; below us Bent Elbow homestead. I see in an instant that Hanna has hung out the wash, that the fruit on the pear tree is coming along, that the woodpile is low, and that Blossom is firmly planted in the middle of the garden, working on the newly set flower bed, picking delicately with her great blunt teeth at the tiny seedlings. Martin sees this too, but it is not Blossom who makes him pull up on Claudius until the wagon comes to a halt.

Martha is walking toward us, climbing the path in her long gait, swinging her sun hat on its string. Walking toward us as if we had all had breakfast together this morning, as if she had nothing more in mind than to call us to table. She waves to us and begins to move faster. Her skirts swing around her calves in a half circle and then swing back again.

Down at the house, Hanna has come outside. She stands there with one hand pressed to her mouth, watching Martha. Watching me.

I begin to raise myself off the seat, and my arm comes

up, all on its own, in response to Martha's wave, but Martin catches it.

Martin catches my arm with his hard hand and pulls it down. He holds on tight, so tight that tomorrow five bruises will arch from my wrist to my elbow.

"Don't," Martin says, and he holds my gaze as tightly as he holds my arm. His eyes are blue, like mine. "Please."

But I do, I look at my sister coming toward us, at her beautiful, shining, trusting face. It wears no hint, no awareness of the heartache that is waiting for her on this wagon seat. I look at Martin. On his face, less serene, a question is clearly written.

And this is the surprise: I thought it would be Martin's choice, Martin's choosing between my sister and me, but the choice turns out to be mine.

Bengat's Olga at the Dairy
1946

TO:
Corporal Klaus Natter
Prisoner No. 2564P.S.
2 Div, Ackenau Artillery Regiment
Odessa, Russia
1 September 1946

Dearest Husband!
     We have been busy in the dairy and in addition we have
had more trouble with Mama, and the cat died. So this letter is
late. With it I will send some dried meat and fruit and a pair of
socks and hope that they get to you.
     First of all I should tell you that our boys and me are well
enough off, although Mama is poorly. I guess you'll want to know
the whole story so I'll start at the beginning.

I was waiting for my loaf at Dokwiese's last Saturday morning when I looked up and there was Jakob, staring back at me from the plate glass window. I never was so surprised. He was wearing the scarf I knit for him before he went off to the war, but he looked real aggravated, and I was about to ask him what was wrong (you remember how sweet Jakob was as a boy, so even tempered) when he just disappeared as quick as he come. And I stood there with my mouth open and Hannelore says to me from behind the counter I looked like I seen a ghost, and I say well I guess I did, Jakob who stepped on a mine in Italy three years ago had just shown himself clear as day in the plate glass window.

And Muxel's Margit who was ahead of me in line let out a big sigh and said well then Olga you better be ready, because when the dead come back it's not for nothing. Hannelore crossed herself and said that's true, they come back to tell you something. Then Wainwright's Katharina came in and we all shut up. People aren't talking to Katharina's face these days although they do enough talking behind her back. Now I try to be Christian and charitable, so I don't join in when the others get started but I can't approve of her ways either.

So all the way home I worried, what did it mean, that Jakob had come back in broad daylight with a scowl on his face. And I was thinking about that so hard that I ran right into the new priest, not looking where I was going. So he asks me what's wrong, and right away I knew that I couldn't just tell him about Jakob showing up in that window, because he is from the Flatlands and he don't even understand our way of talking very well yet and anyway, I knew that he would tell me that the dead don't come back, even in the face of evidence to the contrary. So I just said that my dead brother had been on my mind and he asked which one? and that got me to wondering why Jakob had come back and not Jos or Leo or Tony. But then I remembered Jakob as a baby, once he learned to walk–

you and I were just starting to keep company then–how he never was where he was supposed to be. Aunt Barbara called him a wandering spirit, and it looks to be more true than ever. At any rate I got myself home as quick as I could because there was soup on the stove and I was worried about Mama.

Now Mama had actually had a good night: she spent all of it in her own bed and I didn't have to send the boys out to find her and bring her home, and she didn't wake us up shouting. And when she came to breakfast she didn't ask me first thing where was her boys? When I walked in the kitchen with the bread she was sitting at the table and right away I could see that she had slipped away from us again. Her fingers were picking at her sleeve, she looked confused and she wouldn't talk to me when I asked her what was the matter. Her color was pretty bad, and I wondered if what the Doctor had warned me about was at hand, if Mama's time was close. And that's when it came to me that maybe Jakob had been looking for Mama.

Then Christian came in (he is getting to be such a big boy, now at ten he is wearing the same trousers Alois wore at fifteen) to see did I bring anything from the baker besides bread and Mama looked up and says to him, Jakob, what are you doing in the kitchen when there's cows waiting to be milked. That surely gave me a jolt. And Christian started to remind Mama how this isn't her homestead, how it's his Daddy's, when I hushed him up. Then he rolled his eyes at me and said Ma, you got to do something about this. So I went down to call Alois to table and I took the time to tell him about Jakob and Mama. He just looked real thoughtful for a while, and he kept thinking while he finished tending to the three-month cheeses and then he said in his slow way Ma, don't worry about it too much, if he's got something to tell you, he'll come back. And it struck me that he was right, and that put my mind to rest a little. Soon I guess Alois will be looking for a bride, if he can learn to untie his tongue and ask for what he wants.

Then at dinner we had a terrible lot of noise because young Klaus wanted to bring the cat to the table and I said no and before I could stop him Christian had just reached on over and smacked Klaus hard on the back of the head for even suggesting such a thing. (I am worried about Christian, it seems like he got enough mean bones for all three boys put together.) And Klaus yelped when he felt the knot rising up on his scalp, and Alois took after Christian, and Mama just sat in the middle of it all as if she was stone deaf. It is times like this I miss you most at our table.

Things were so busy in the afternoon that I just didn't have time to think about Jakob. So when he showed up he took me by surprise again, this time when I opened the door to our wardrobe to put up the ironing and there he was in the mirror, but way off in the corner. When I turned around quick he was gone already. So it seemed the sensible thing was to go to Saturday evening mass, which I did, and said prayers for the dead for all my brothers, thinking it might calm Jakob down to know he weren't forgot. Then I stayed a good time at my family grave and yours. (Last week it was four years since Mikatrin's Maria drowned. She has planted a new rosebush.)

The whole time I wondered who might show themselves, thinking maybe Jakob had not come all that way alone. But nobody did, so I went home. And that's when I found the cat lying in a heap in front of the door, already cold. It occurs to me now you wouldn't even know which cat I was talking about. It was the white one Jakob set such a store by, he come by with it on his shoulder the day he left for the war, and Klaus was so struck with the idea of Uncle Jakob going when the other Uncles were already gone and Jos and Tony dead already (and Leo too but we didn't know that then) that he just went all white and still. But Jakob put the cat in Klaus's lap and said never mind about me, just take care of the cat because I'll come back for her when the war is over, she's your responsibility. So

all the worry about Mama and it seemed that Jakob had come
back for his cat. Although it still don't explain the sour look on
his face. And this was a relief and an aggravation too, because
Klaus thought the sun rose and set on that cat, and what was
he going to say? Or I guess I was worried he'd never say another
word again. I'd of guessed it wasn't possible for a boy to be quiet-
er than Alois, but young Klaus sure tries hard. It is worrisome.

Now Klaus I can hear you telling me Olga don't encour-
age our boys to be sentimental about the animals, but the fact
is, if we are going to give over farming to make cheese full time,
and take on everybody's milk, then that makes us a *Sennhaus*
and a dairy needs a cat. I have never seen a single mouse drop-
ping near the butterfat tubs since she came to us. And I was
fond of her too I admit, she was an affectionate thing, and knew
just when a body was feeling low. She'd got the habit of sitting
in my lap while I knit, evenings.

So there I was with a dead cat in my arms and no idea
what to tell Klaus when Alois came to meet me at the door and
say he had sent Christian down to Ackenau to fetch the Doctor,
Mama seemed to be in a bad way. Then I didn't know what to
think anymore, had Jakob come back to help Mama on her way
and taken the cat as an after thought, or the other way around?
I was worried sick about Mama and wanted to get up to her
right away and still I didn't want young Klaus to stumble on
this dead animal. So I gave it to Alois to hide in the bushes and
hoped a fox wouldn't come after it before I could bury it.

And right away I could see how things were with Mama,
one side of her face sagging and her right arm lying at her side
like a piece of wood, and I knew that Doctor Troy weren't going
to be any help. But what went through my mind most of all, I
have already confessed it but I feel I must tell you as well, was
at least we won't have to worry about her wandering through
the village at night no more. I was ashamed of that thought
when it came to me, but the priest seemed to understand, what

with the Moroccan soldiers hanging around at all hours, and he couldn't see the sin in it. Which was a relief. The Doctor got Mama settled as comfortable as she was going to be and told me how to look after her and to come fetch him if there was any change at all, and then on his way out he turned to me and took my hands and said Olga, you've had some tough times in the past few years and maybe worse is to come. Your Mama could hang on like this for a long time.

In the middle of the night young Klaus came into Mama's room where I was sitting next to her. His voice was all hoarse and shaky, wanting to know could he go look for his cat, he couldn't get to sleep without knowing was she all right. Sometimes it feels like everything comes down on a person at once.

Finally I got him calmed down and sent him back to bed and when I thought he must be asleep I woke Christian and told him to sit with Mama. Then I woke Alois and together we went down to the garden to bury that cat. Alois dug a hole in the far corner under the apple tree and we laid her in. First I remember thinking what prayer would be suitable for a cat and then I thought maybe this grave will be a comfort to the boy, knowing where she lies. Lord knows Mama wouldn't be where she is now if she could have put her own boys to rest where they belong in the family grave, instead of thinking of them, all four, in foreign soil where no one knows them or cares for them, not to mention the cousins still missing and no word since they were taken from River's Bend in '38. And I was thinking about that when I looked up and there was young Klaus standing at the window, watching us, and the moonlight bright on the body of his cat, her fur shining like silver.

So that's the story I wanted to tell you. Mama's still hanging on, like Doctor Troy said. She can't hold her water and she dirties herself like a baby, but she lies there sweet as one too, looking at me with the same trust our boys had in their eyes when they were new and I was everything in the world to them.

Young Klaus went looking for his cat the next day, he looked for her for two days, and I started to wonder if maybe I had dreamed the whole thing, him at the window looking down at Alois and me. I was so distracted with Mama I just could not bring myself to take young Klaus aside and show him the grave, but Alois did it, without my asking.

Every day I go to the baker for our loaf and I watch that glass window. I wonder if Jakob will show himself again, or if the cat was all he was after. I wonder if the others will come back to claim what they left behind, one at a time. I wonder if I will ever look up and see you there, and if you will seem as far away to me as you do now, or if you might smile at me and hold out your hand.

Every night and every morning we pray that you are well. Although now in the heat of the summer I don't have to worry about whether you've got a blanket or if you've got frostbite. Again with this letter I will try to send you a small cheese, although I fear it will not get through the way things are in the East.

Folks here abouts are pretty tired of being occupied. We pray every Sunday morning that these French and Moroccans will go away and let us get on with our business. Gretel from the Hill, who was once courted by our Jos, is going to marry a farmer with a big homestead out in the valley. Dokwiese's Harald who kept the clock at the factory fell down some steps and broke his hip the other day. I won't deny that I was glad to see the end of him when I left the factory, but it seems a harsh punishment, after all.

The schoolteacher from Vienna went back home last month (some story about his Mama needing him) and Martha moved back into the quarters in the schoolhouse right away. I guess she was relieved to get away from Bent Elbow, as things are getting crowded out there these days—the Cobbler's Youngest has fathered a fine big boy and got another child well started since he married Mikatrin. Mikatrin comes to the village twice a week to fetch butter and whey, and passes a few minutes with me. We talk about the old days, when she and Leo were keeping company and sometimes they would come out to Bengat on a summer's evening. And you and me would go over too and Jos and Tony would get out the guitars and we would sing, do you remember? Until Daddy would say time to get on to bed, the cows wouldn't give any more milk for having been serenaded til morning.

At night a cold wind comes down off the First Sister. It don't seem possible that another summer is almost gone. Pretty soon the livestock will be on the road down from high alp.

I have been considering telling the new priest about the cat, to see if there's some prayer I might still say over her.

It has been near a year and a half now since I have had word from you. When the boys are asleep I sit at the kitchen table with my knitting and watch the window and the road, hoping to catch some sight of you, any sight at all.

Your loving wife,
Olga

Alois's Katharina at the Dairy
1950

Dairy Alois's Katharina, once known as Wainwright's Katharina, known for a shorter time as the Moroccan's Whore, leaves home on the day her nephew Stante comes back from the dead.

It is the last Sunday in March, and her husband's birthday. She has set the table in the *Stube* with her best linen. From her spot on top of the console radio, the carved Madonna looks on with grim approval as Katharina puts beef broth with semolina dumplings, veal roast, buttered carrots and red cabbage with apples, and potatoes in gravy before her daughter and husband, her husband's brothers and mother.

When there is nothing left but empty platters and dishes, Olga helps her daughter-in-law clear the table. Lilimarlene, three years old, must have her part of the woman's work: she carries the dirty soup spoons to the kitchen at arm's length, mindful of her good dirndl of checked pink and its matching apron.

Alois sits at the table with his brothers to either side. When Klaus and Christian come to Sunday dinner there is always an argument, but their talk has slowed down now that they are sated. They blink drowsily at one another. They let today's quarrel run down and sputter away.

Katharina sends Olga and Lilimarlene back to the table so she can see to dessert without having them underfoot; to get a minute to herself. The kitchen is heavy with cooking smells, and she takes the time to open a window and lean out over the snowy garden. A cold wind pushes past her; she likes the feel of it on her flushed face and she leans her elbows on the sill and puts her chin in her hands.

It is a beautiful afternoon, in the sharp way the latest winter days are sometimes too clear, too bright. The sky is divided in half by the diagonal of the church roof, and behind it the mountain snowfields are pearl and blue-gray shadows. Late at night Katharina sometimes hears rumblings from the Three Sisters as winter's grip loosens; she can see the fissures in the snowfields creeping and deepening day by day. Soon the avalanches will start.

Katharina feels the skin on her cheeks tighten with the cold, or with tears wanting to come; she can't tell which.

Every morning Katharina tells Alois what she will need that day from the dairy: how much cream, milk, butter, whey, cheese. He measures it out, makes a note in the cooperative books to his account, and brings it up when the morning's work is done. But when she has spooned the compote into her best bowls, Katharina realizes there is no cream.

She stands in her bright clean kitchen and she ponders this, the strange and unanticipated lack of cream, until Lilimarlene wanders in with her thumb in her mouth. The child is tired, and she mumbles and rubs her dirty face against Katharina's skirt. Katharina does not push her away. She just does not have the energy to stand up to Lilimarlene, who was born to do battle with her mother. Instead she puts a hand on Lilimarlene's dark head, her sleek dark head with its small ears and wide-set hazel eyes, and she rubs the child's temple until Lilimarlene sighs with contentment and almost falls asleep against Katharina's leg.

When Alois came calling with marriage on his mind, it wasn't because he didn't know about the baby on the way, but because he did. He had always had his eye on Katharina, and for once he had the advantage: what was she going to do, after all? Other women stayed at home to raise their mistakes: Kasparle's Gret for example, who had a daughter by somebody she didn't care to name, or Annobüobli's Rudolf's youngest, who went off to visit her sister down in Ackenau and came back carrying her brother-in-law's child.

Alois was a man with steady work and no livestock to look after; he could have had Gret, or any of the spinsters or war widows. Katharina knew she would do no better. Not with the growing bulge under her skirt, not since the man who put it there had left with the rest of the occupation troops. So she married Alois, the Wainwright less than six months in his grave: more gossip.

There is a photo of Lilimarlene's father that Katharina has hidden away; she rarely looks at it these days. Half French and half Moroccan, Katharina's Moor, folks called him. Rhymes and jokes had been made up. What do you get when you cross a hussy and a Moor? A whoooor. They drew the word out and out. Now Katharina looks at Lilimarlene and sees her Moor, with hair just like this, like Lilimarlene's. His hands were long-fingered, his nails perfect ovals. The things Katharina remembers about him are few: his pockets were always full of almonds, wrinkled cigarette papers, bandage scissors, bits of gauze; he had a serious taste for the local schnapps and a melodious and surprisingly deep singing voice.

Katharina sends Lilimarlene back into the *Stube* to sit on

Alois's lap until dessert is ready. Then she takes a jug and puts on her sweater and goes downstairs, past Alois's certificates from the agricultural school and the cheesemaker's guild. The strong smell of hundreds of liters of heated milk meets her halfway down. Her heels click on the tiles–yellow, blue, yellow, blue–as she walks to the cooler and through it to get to the cream vat.

She opens it with one hand and gasps. There is a mouse rolling gently in the thick cream, a sleek gray form coated deep white, the tail curled delicately into a question mark. Katharina lets the lid fall shut, turns on heel, and leaves the cooler. She goes to the window that looks out on the lane and toward the church square.

Katharina is thinking of the last year of the war. How there was so little of anything, how people started making their own cheese again and hiding it away, spinning excuses to the requisitions officer for the decrease in milk. How folks snuck in from the cities to buy what they could, desperate for a few eggs, a bit of cheese, a kilo of venison shot on the sly. Willing to trade filigreed earrings, crackly old paintings, silver spoons rainbowed with tarnish. How the Wainwright died with his empty coffee cup cradled to his chest, whining and whining for chicory with cream when even ersatz coffee was more precious than cash and it was worth your skin to lift the thick from the milk before you turned it over to the military.

In that last year of the war how surprised she was to see that some things she thought everlasting–milk, her father, the war itself–also had their limitations.

Upstairs her husband is waiting. Her kind husband, with his mild brown eyes and milder expectations. It is his birthday, and there are apricots she put up in the summer, and later there will be coffee and the cake she baked late last night. People are surprised that she has turned out a good housewife. Sometimes something old and ornery in her wants to prove them right, and then she is tempted to hang out stained linen and buy canned vegetables, knowing that these things would not surprise anybody: it is what they want of her. But in the night, when she can't sleep, Katharina turns her hand to the house, to the laundry, to anything at all that is excuse enough to keep the lights burning.

She should go upstairs, but she dreads what will happen. If she serves her compote without cream, Alois will remember and come down here and find the mouse, and the rest of the day will be spent scrubbing every pail and vat, putting out traps, checking lard and cheese, hunting down the nest where the foolish creature made its bed or the crack where it came in from the field. Katharina thinks of it hiding away in its nest, where it was safe but hungry. She wonders at it, that a mouse could show enough determination to find its way into Alois's cream vat, only to learn that a full stomach made turning back treacherous.

It occurs to Katharina that she could at least put the outcry off if she borrows some cream. She could walk just across the church square and get some from her half sister, slip in and out before they know she's gone. Moving fast, with the cream jug in one hand, Katharina opens the heavy metal door to step into the bright afternoon. She shivers in her sweater, her shoulders hunched, as she hurries down the snowy path.

Katharina runs up the stone steps and into the house where she grew up, her wet shoes slipping a little on the crackly linoleum in the hallway. To her right is the open door to the shop, empty and shuttered on a Sunday. "Ho-la!" she calls out, and "Ho-la!" again, and in reply she hears a sharp shout of laughter.

She finds them in the kitchen huddled around the table, cards spread before them: her mother, Grumpy Marie, and Bengat's Barbara, deep in their *Jass* game.

"Short of cream," Katharina says, glad to see them so distracted that they won't ask for an explanation.

Marie jerks her head toward the other end of the house; in the winter she unplugs the refrigerator and keeps things cold in the abandoned smithy. "Help yourself," she says, and slaps down a card with a little grunt of satisfaction.

Katharina watches them for a minute. They have pulled the overhead lamp down low on its chain, and it shines on thin braids of silver and peppery white. Three old women hunched over fans of cards clutched between knobby fingers.

Every Sunday Barbara comes up from River's Bend for mass and stays to play cards at the Wainwright's. Folks think it is because Barbara cannot go without her weekly *Jass*, but Katharina knows better: she comes because these three have the Wainwright in common. For the four years he has been dead they come together on Sunday afternoons to prove it to themselves, as if their combined force of will might just keep him in his grave. Just as the veterans sit in the Eagle over their beer to pass the war back and forth, a possession too awful to ignore, better shared than digested in solitude.

Katharina looks closely at her mother and sees that Theres has decided not to take notice of her. Theres's eyes are fixed solidly on her cards, her mouth folded tight in concentration. This is a great relief, and Katharina feels the muscles of her shoulders loosening a little. It is rare for Katharina to be in her mother's company without triggering one of Theres's monologues. And the room is warm, and Barbara smiles at Katharina, and so she tarries a minute.

The household shrine presides over the table where they play their game, the corner crucifix angled out above the triangular shelf that bridges the gap where the high-backed benches come together. There, three wooden figurines have been arranged shoulder to shoulder on a linen cloth edged in lace: the Madonna balanced on a world, the serpent wrapped around her ankles; Saint Christopher, his eyes rolling upward as if he cannot bear the scent of the dried flowers at his feet;

and Saint John looking boyish and puzzled, unable to make sense of the fan of holy cards so carefully propped against his robes. Mourning cards, all of them, each bearing a grainy black-and-white likeness: Rosenau's dead–old folks, soldiers serene in their uniforms, pale children–assembled here to demand daily prayers for their souls. Bent Elbow's Angelika on top, hollow-cheeked and wild-eyed, the cancer showing there. *Beloved mother, dutiful wife, cherished sister called home to Glory.*

Above all this, hung at an angle from low ceiling to wall so that they look down on the table, larger likenesses of the family dead: Old Woman, Grumpy Marie's mother, gone almost sixty years now and her sepia image fading fast: *He has claimed her for His own.* The Wainwright, his eyebrows wiry twists of iron gray, his scowl burning down as if he begrudged every bite of food taken at the table without his say-so: *A long and fruitful life.* Katharina's nephews. Michel looking almost normal, his head not quite so crooked as usual, Stante's shy eyes, the muscular neck straining at his collar. Konstantin and Michel Metzler, 1901-1938: *Innocent lambs*, in spindly black script below. *Taken from us.*

The room is quiet except for the sound of breathing and the fluttering of the cards. The women seem to have forgotten Katharina standing there; Katharina seems to have forgotten how to move. She finds herself floating above the old women, removed somehow and looking down on the scene, suspended up there with the rest of the dead, the light too bright on the oil-cloth. This is not so bad, she thinks to herself, seeing her own body down below her, the white cream jug clutched in one hand. Seeing her own face, pale; she is not startled to see her daughter's face outlined so clearly there.

Then Theres looks up suddenly as if she senses her daughter hovering above her; a little shudder passes through her.

With a jolt Katharina is back on the ground in her damp

shoes. She has aroused her mother's attention; it is too late to run.

There are splashes of color on Theres's cheeks and neck. She stares at her daughter indignantly. "Looking at your cousins, are you? Thinking about the twins?"

Marie looks up. "Don't start, Theres."

"Those boys are dead and gone, Theres," Barbara says in a weary tone. "Let's leave them in peace."

"You don't know that," Theres snaps. Her eyes dare anyone to take up this battle, anyone at all will do: but she would prefer Katharina. She would like to say out loud once again what everybody else thinks but keeps to themselves.

"It's not like you ever had a spare word for them when they were alive," Marie mutters.

Theres's face shifts a little, so that under her high color and bright eyes Katharina sees what is left of her mother, and what is coming. Barbara sees it too, and she sends Katharina a compassionate look.

"She should have stayed with them," Theres says to Grumpy Marie. Her mouth curves down, a thin line in her face. "They needed her to show them the way home."

Marie is looking at Katharina, waiting for her to stand up for herself, stand up to her mother. If Katharina could do that, just stop all this by saying for once *shut up you stupid old bitch*—a sentence that repeats itself in her head again and again whenever she is with her mother—then Marie would know how to come to her aid. But Katharina has never been able to do anything but accept her mother's bitterness; she has nothing to say in her own defense. She never has. Because about this one thing her mother is right, and Katharina knows it.

Although it is very tidy and clean, Katharina does not like the smithy. She doesn't like the emptiness of it, the tools hung in such order on their pegs, the rust on the anvil. The quiet. The oil-stained floor swept clean. For a long time after the Nazi came to take the twins away, twelve years ago now, the smithy stayed just as it was: the Wainwright refused to believe that Stante was gone, and wouldn't let anybody mess with the work he had left half done. Then the Wainwright died and the smithy fell to Grumpy Marie's care.

The door stands half open, as it always does. Snow skitters in lazily across the floor in a puff of wind. Katharina's hands are shaking a little, and she rubs them together before she starts pouring cream from Marie's jug into her own.

A shadow falls across the step and she looks up.

An old man stands there kneading a battered cap between his fingers. The sun is at his back and his face is hard to make out. He has a large head, with hair shaved close to the scalp, gray from what she can see. There is something funny about his posture; he is crumpled together like a wad of paper.

"Can I help you?" she says, her voice coming out all strained and unfamiliar.

He steps forward a little; his gaze keeps falling and rising, from the floor to her face and back again. His eyes are very blue.

"The shop is closed," Katharina says, but gently now. The soft hair at the nape of her neck is rising.

Finally he focuses his gaze on her and she is able to see him clearly: a long face, a strong nose and chin, a well-defined mouth. His tongue sweeps out to wet his lower lip.

"Stante," Katharina says.

And his face breaks into a smile.

"Stante," she says again.

He shuffles forward, nodding at her, grinning. She steps back. He stops in front of the table where she has been pouring the cream; his eyes move over the bits of cheese wrapped in oiled paper, the lump of butter.

Katharina's heart is racing. She can feel the blood pumping through her in great panicked rushes, flooding her face, setting her hands to tingling. The room darkens a little; she pinches the flesh between thumb and first finger hard until her sight clears.

"Where's Michel?" she asks, and is surprised when this question comes out of her mouth, as if someone else had put it there.

Stante leans over the cheese box and with two claw-like fingers grabs a small chunk that has been pared almost to the rind; he glances furtively at Katharina as if he expects her to take it away from him.

"Where's your brother?" Katharina repeats.

"Dead," Stante says, and he pops the rind into his mouth.

They recognize him right away. The three of them flutter and stumble all over each other and him. Katharina stands back and tries not to watch.

"You see!" Theres is saying again and again, triumphant. "You see! You see!"

Grumpy Marie, more agitated than Katharina has ever before seen her, thumps bread down on the table; Stante reaches for it with one hand while the other moves his soup spoon in a steady rhythm from plate to mouth. Barbara and Marie are shooting questions at each other and at him, getting no answers, asking more questions anyway.

Suddenly Theres turns to her daughter. "Go get the priest," she says.

This causes Grumpy Marie to take note. "What for? We don't need the priest."

"The priest," says Theres stubbornly. "It's a miracle, the priest should be here."

"Katharina," says Barbara. "Your mother-in-law should be here. She's his first cousin. Too bad Anna didn't live to see this day," she adds, looking at Stante.

"The priest," says Theres again.

"Will you be quiet with your priest," snaps Grumpy Marie.

"The doctor is more like it. Go get Dr. Troy. Have a look at this boy, see what's up."

Katharina nods, at all of them, at none of them, and she turns to leave, glad of this excuse to get out.

"Trina," says Stante; she stops.

They all turn to him. Soup runs down a chin rough with gray stubble. His blue eyes are bright and eager. He is glad to be here, glad to be home.

But he doesn't have anything else to say to Katharina. All the things she imagined him saying over the years are just not there. He smiles at her briefly, as if it is only a matter of days since he has seen her last. Then he falls to his soup again.

"Can you tell us where you've been all these years?" Barbara says to him. "And what happened to Michel? What did they do to you?"

Stante glances at Katharina over his spoon, and then at Barbara. One of his hands creeps down to his lap, and Katharina sees that he is squeezing himself under the table, a convulsive twist of the hand. There is a confused and distraught look on his face.

"He'll talk, just let him get his stomach full," says Grumpy Marie.

And Katharina knows that this is true: that he will talk, that he will tell them what happened to him and how Michel died and what it was like, all of it. As Katharina leaves the kitchen, her mother calls after her.

"All for a ride in a motorcar!" she yells.

Katharina walks to the hallway, the cream forgotten. Marie's good cloak hangs on the wall with her boots underneath; she puts these on. The pockets are full: damp wool gloves, some coins, a half bar of chocolate. Without looking back, Katharina walks down the steps in the bright sunshine, narrowing her eyes a little in the glare. Farmers take naps on Sunday afternoons; the church square is empty.

She turns down the lane that leads out of the square and eventually drops away down the mountainside to Ackenau. Dr. Troy has built a house on the Low Road between the two villages to save himself trouble. It is a new house that Katharina has heard a lot about, although she has never seen it. But she knows what to look for, and so she sets off down the lane with her head bowed, feeling the village huddled behind her.

She passes homestead after homestead; once or twice she catches a glimpse of a face at a *Stube* window. There is a faint rumbling where the First and Second Sisters lean together; then a louder rush of engine noise and the yellow *Bundespost* coach comes lumbering up the road on its solitary Sunday run.

In just a minute Katharina expects to come to the Big Curve, and from there she should be able to see Dr. Troy's house. Stucco and carved wooden balconies. She imagines the fine lace at the windows, the mural painted on the wall facing the road. Dr. Troy will be surprised to see her. His wife will wake him from his nap, and he will come to the door smoothing his great unruly mustache and raise an eyebrow when he sees who it is. Alois's Katharina, he will think, how odd. And he will want to know what she needs, who is in trouble.

Katharina pauses in the road, and the silence strikes her. She shuffles Marie's boots in the loosening snow, and there seems to be no noise at all.

What will she tell him? That Stante has come back from the dead. That twelve years ago she drove down this mountainside between him and his twin and listened to them crying and then watched them led away without saying a word. That anybody you cared to ask in Rosenau would tell you what everybody believed: the boys had been burned up in one of those camps the Nazis built, and they would never come back again, and Katharina had been the last one to see them. That she had let them go without a blessing, without a goodbye, without a tear, and raced back home herself, as fast as she could, until every muscle in her screamed out in protest. That her mother—who to that very day had not spoken more than five words a week—started talking, but could talk only about the boys.

He is a good doctor; he doesn't complain about Sunday visits and he is gentle. When the midwife had the influenza he delivered Lilimarlene humming the whole time. Katharina has a memory of him standing between her thighs, chewing on one end of his mustache, a swipe of blood on his cheek.

So she'll tell him that Stante has come home. As simple as that. Stante has found his way back from the dead.

The doctor will come up to the village with her; she imagines him standing in the kitchen, where Old Woman and the Wainwright will look down from their death notices to watch him poke and prod Stante, listen to his heart, ask him to drop his trousers to see if the rumors are true, if the Nazis did to feeble-minded men what farmers did to bulls too stupid or weak or bow-legged to breed. She can see Barbara, her face grim and pale; she can see Grumpy Marie; she can hear her mother.

While she stands there thinking of what her mother will have to say, of Stante with his trousers around his ankles and three old women looking on over the doctor's shoulders, the village waiting to hear, the coach comes roaring back down the road and stops. The door opens.

"Running late," the driver says. "Sorry." He is a big man, maybe fifty years old; he is missing two fingers on his right hand, and there is a scar under his left eye.

Katharina steps up into the coach. He pulls the lever that shuts the door. The coach is empty. Katharina takes a seat behind the driver and looks back up the road toward the church square. She can see the corner of the dairy, a bit of the bedroom window where Alois will sleep tonight. If she cranes her head she can see another window, with birds of brightly colored paper taped to the glass. She turns her head away.

"Off we go," the driver says, and the coach moves on. "You for Ackenau?" he asks Katharina without taking his eyes from the road.

On the other side of the stream River's Bend flashes by; they take a curve and Dr. Troy's new house comes and goes.

"I haven't been to Ackenau for twelve years," Katharina says, mostly to herself.

"Then it's about time," the driver laughs.

The road is slick; underneath the coach the snow chains grip, jingling like a pocketful of coins. Around and behind them the snowfields cradled on the slopes of the Praying Hands groan and shift in the growing warmth of the sun. Katharina hears them, but she never turns back.

Martha

Rosenau School 1959

I keep the school in this village. Every child born here comes into my classroom. Most of them will grow up to spend their lives looking after the land, but they won't do so in ignorance: these children learn to write legibly, draw a map of Africa, multiply and divide fractions, and recite the poems of Goethe and Rilke. They understand the life cycle of the white thorn and the oak and the habits of the birds who live in them.

The children stay with me until I am satisfied they are ready to move on; some are here a good while. Over the years I have had a few special children who need more than I can give them. They go to board at one of the schools in Bregenz or Dornbirn, and from there on to university or college. But those children learned their letters from me, and I claim them as my own: I have an engineer, two priests, a nursing sister, and a teacher of geography and history to my credit so far. All of them have left Rosenau for good, but they write to me.

Every morning at ten o'clock, I send my children out to breathe our mountain air. I stand at the door and I watch them at play. This is when they reveal their true selves to me: their weaknesses and strengths, their hidden soft places and scaly spots, the mistakes they will make over and over again in this life.

Kasparle's Laura, who sits there reading while the others are busy jumping rope, she's one who will always want something different. I know the look, because I wore it myself as a child.

Laura keeps herself separate not so much because the other children don't like her or want to play with her, or because she's too pretty for comfort, but because it's what she expects of herself. Since her mother died, Laura has been living on her uncle's homestead, the biggest and grandest farm in the village. Her great-grandfather was Ackenau's farmer-poet, the man we hold up to outsiders as proof of a worthy heritage. These things alone would be enough to set Laura apart, but the fact is she's got no father, never has had—that is a rare and valuable currency for an intelligent child. Without it, Laura would have no excuse but to be like the others. Laura doesn't know who her father was. I would claim that she is more fortunate than I am: she needn't pretend she does.

The summer I was nineteen years old, my father—the man I called my father—looked up with a rankled expression and died in mid-swing of the scythe, putting an end to a year-long argument about whether or not he could afford to send me away to school. Two days after we buried him, Mama started getting my clothes in order while my godmother Johanna drove our third-best milch cow and the old brood sow to town. She bargained until there was enough money to send me to Innsbruck in time for the start of the fall semester at the teacher's college.

Some weeks later, on a clear morning when Innsbruck's ring of stern mountain wall was marbled with early snow, I attended my first biology lecture, which was entitled "The Mystery of the Seed: Gregor Johann Mendel's Laws of Heredity." In the course of that hour I learned that blue eye color is a recessive trait and that two blond, blue-eyed people, such as my parents were, have no option but to produce offspring with eyes and coloring like their own.

That night, as I looked in the polished metal mirror above my sink at eyes and hair the color of black walnut, it became clear to me that the only mysteries that really mattered were back at the Bent Elbow homestead, waiting to be solved.

As a girl with nothing so concrete as an unknown father to hang my eccentricities on, I had overlooked the clues: a sister who was the negative image of myself–pale blond with eyes the color of a hot summer sky, and a temperament quick to storm; the talent I had for schooling, which our father met with skepticism and suspicion.

My father's distance might have been harder on me if it hadn't been for my mother and godmother, who tussled constantly for my favor but hotly denied any partiality. They were two dignified women caught in an undignified guerrilla war, and my smile was the prize. I took shameless advantage of their imperfect love.

They loved me so well that later I found I could not settle for less. To start with, I didn't have to. The first man I loved was the best, but he fell in the war. I might have married in the end, but most of the young men my age died in France or North Africa or at Stalingrad. Those who came back found wives who would farm beside them. They raised families, and in time they sent their children to my school. Every day at ten I send those children out to play, and they reveal themselves to me.

Just across from the school is the little house I had built back in 1950. Godmother sits in the *Schopf* and watches the children play from behind a low wall of geraniums; she has done this every school day since she moved in with me the summer the house was finished. She sits there all seasons, in spite of what the chill does to eighty-year-old bones brittle as sugar candy. In the deep of winter her blue eyes, still clear and over-sharp, water with the cold, and tears run down her ruddy cheeks.

The mountains are shimmering with autumn. There are great rustlings of color, brighter this year than for many years past. The sky clutches, ready to give way to winter; any time now my sister and her family will drive the livestock down from fall pasture at Gunta Steeple and back to the homestead at Bent Elbow. Then my nephews will return to my classroom, and at recess Laura will have to make room at Godmother's knee for one or two or all five at once. The children sit with Hanna because she is a natural-born storyteller. Her secret, I have observed, is that she does not give her stories away cheaply. She makes those children earn them; she doles them out like the treasures they are.

Sometimes, on a winter night when she stares out into the dark and listens, I think that the time has come and she will tell me what I have waited so long to hear, the circumstances of my conception in the summer of 1916, during the Great War.

In 1938 I rushed home from Innsbruck with my new teaching certificate, armed with painstakingly worded questions, ready to battle my mother for the answers. But I found Mama busy with a war of her own: her cancer disarmed me immediately but took a few months longer to wear her down to nothing.

On the last day of her life, when I was alone with her for a few minutes, I took her hand and asked her to tell me about my father.

"The war soured Hans," she said as if she had been waiting for this question. "He was never cruel as a young man."

So she left me and took the truth with her.

In time, I would have thought to turn to Hanna and ask her, but before I had a chance another war had started, and when that war was done with me I had lost my taste for the truth. It was many years before I thought with any interest or curiosity about the color of my eyes.

Mama was not a storyteller; I have forgiven her for that, finally. It is for Godmother to tell, I hope. Although at times I fear that the price she asks for that story will be very high.

During afternoon recitation the sound of animals on the move pulls the children out of their seats as the Gunta Steeple folks drive the livestock past the school windows. This is the last *Vorschaß* to come down this season, so I let them leave their desks to watch.

My sister leads. Her oldest boy, Martin, and her second-youngest, Rudi, are on either side of her. Her husband, also Martin, brings up the rear on horseback, the youngest of the boys in front of him on the saddle. Martin's wooden leg is stuck in a bucket-like contraption that serves as a stirrup. The middle two boys, almost identical in their brown skins and white-blondness, are scattered among the animals, wielding their sticks casually and prancing for their schoolmates, old cowhands. It would be an unforgivable breach of dignity for them to wave at us, but my sister does. Mikatrin smiles at me and lifts her hat.

To this day, Mikatrin believes that she took Martin away from me. She has always had me a little bit out of focus, which may be irritating at times, but it also provides me with an unusual amount of freedom: the mistakes and faults she ascribes to me are not as painful as the ones that are truly my own. Mikatrin doesn't feel guilty about what she thinks she did; she had her reasons, and most of them she could list out loud and feel no shame.

Now that they are home again, Godmother will be out of sorts and impatient for the rest of the week, when we will have our Sunday dinner at Bent Elbow.

149

After mass I hitch up Caesar and we set off. On our way through the church square, the boys come running to hurl themselves into the back of the wagon for the ride up to the homestead, whooping and hollering to each other and to their friends who have the misfortune to live right in the village. For a long time I have been thinking of buying a little car, but then it occurs to me that I would miss this Sunday ride as much as my nephews, and so I put it off.

Godmother shines, sitting above the commotion of boys with her good cape wrapped around her and her peaked Sunday hat perched straight on her crown of braids. Her hands rest on the knob of her cane. There is still something of her old suppleness in them, despite the knotty joints and slightly blue fingernails. She murmurs and Caesar obeys her. It doesn't matter whose hands hold the reins when he hears her voice. It's the same with the children: Hanna knows how to talk to wild things.

Mikatrin and Martin have been to early mass, and when we roll in, spilling boys in every direction, a huge Sunday dinner is on the table. Over a clear soup thick with dumplings we catch up on the six weeks they have been away. Hanna asks about the fall season at alp, about the animals and the new calves and the tractor Martin wants to buy. We talk about farming because farming is all they know; they don't ask about school or the village. It has always been that way since they married. They don't need anything or anyone but themselves and this homestead.

Martin is silent when Mikatrin brings up the topic of the alp at Gunta Steeple. She talks of split shingles, cramped living quarters, the outdated *Stadel*. I imagine that he is displeased with his wife for raising this subject again, but he bites his tongue and bides his time; that is why they are well suited.

The boys put down their knives and forks. They are

expecting a loud argument, the kind that happens almost without fail when Godmother and Mikatrin sit together at this table. Hanna will lose her temper, as she does when Mikatrin starts talking about tearing down the old place to rebuild it. Mikatrin will rise to meet her.

The fact is, half of Gunta Steeple belongs to Godmother, and without her consent there's nothing Mikatrin can do. Nevertheless, she lays out her arguments again, punctuating them with sharp taps of her finger on the tabletop.

Hanna waits for her to finish. Then, to our complete surprise, she smiles.

"Come spring you can do what you want with the alp." She lowers her chin and looks us over, every one. "But first I'm going to winter up there. By myself."

Mikatrin nearly chokes on her carrots, but now that this is out, I am calm. For a while it has been clear to me that Godmother is up to something.

The boys are looking between Martin and Mikatrin uneasily, waiting for one or the other to speak: their father, who will be composed and sensible; their mother, who will wind up and explode in a flurry of words like glass splinters.

"There's firewood for about eight weeks of cold weather," Martin says, matter-of-fact. "A good amount of lamp oil."

"Tomorrow Fellele's Willi is going up to chop wood and stack it. He'll stay the week and he'll take care of any repairs need doing, too," says Hanna.

"What about food?" Jok asks with cheeks full of noodles.

"I got enough preserved meat and dried fruit, and a wheel of cheese, and cornmeal and flour and potatoes and onions."

"You're fond of milk," the younger Martin points out, clearly worried that Hanna might have to do without.

"I expect I can buy a goat easy enough." She smiles, and puts a hand on his head.

Mikatrin is looking back and forth between Godmother

and me, her outrage barely in check. "I suppose you want to send all that up in the new gondola."

Godmother raises an eyebrow. "Well, the goat will walk, I expect."

The two older boys drop their heads as if on cue, because to laugh now would be a terrible mistake. I know the picture they are drawing for themselves. They see a nanny goat peeking out over the edge of the gondola's bucket as it sways gently on its cable on the way up between the First and Second Sisters to the alp. This is a funny idea, no denying it, and I cannot keep my smile hidden.

My sister turns to me, glaring. "Where'd the money come from?"

"Don't look at Martha," Godmother says, raising a crooked finger. "It's the first she's heard of it. I'll tell you where I got the money. I saved it, every last schilling. It's took me forty years, but I done it all myself."

Martin clears his throat. "We can't come after you if something goes wrong."

There's a tic in Mikatrin's cheek. "You'll up and die and we won't be able to get to you till spring," she spits out.

"In that case you can bury me right there," Hanna says, and she reaches for another helping of potatoes.

The move is set for the next Saturday afternoon.

On Monday, Mikatrin comes by after doing her shopping to suggest that the first snow might fall before Saturday; that would keep Hanna where she belongs. On Tuesday, she catches up with me in the cemetery after evening mass to tell me that both the radio and the almanac promise a cold front for the next day. On Wednesday, warm and sunny, she has business at the dairy and comes by the school just as I am heading home for lunch; she wants to know if the priest or Dr. Troy might be able to talk Hanna out of this foolishness. On Thursday, still unseasonably warm for early October, she goes to see Hanna while I am teaching. I watch her go in as recess is ending; she is gone when I get home at noon, and Godmother is serene.

All this time Martin is busy sending supplies up to the Steeple in the gondola. This is not what Mikatrin had in mind when she plotted and saved for that gondola, not at all. I imagine that every time Martin cranks it up with another load of provisions for Godmother, she is torn right in half between pride and aggravation.

On the other end Willi, the hired hand, unloads it all. He spends the rest of his time chopping and stacking firewood, mending the roof and stove, digging a new ditch for the outhouse just beyond the stable entrance, and drinking a good deal. We know about the work he does because he sends down a note in the gondola's empty bucket after the last run of the day; we know about the schnapps by the stains on the paper and the shaky hand. Willi was one of my first students; I didn't do well by him, it seems.

Hanna is not idle. Every day she surprises me by revealing another hidden cache: a huge stack of newspapers and magazines, some of them ten years old; three jars of gooseberry preserves; a new pack of cards; an unopened bottle of aspirin; several tins of matches; a sewing kit; a packet of camomile and one of fennel for tea; a magnifying glass; some books, one with warped covers.

"What book is that?" I ask, leaning over to have a look. *The Mythology of Ancient Rome.* She snatches it out from under my nose, flushing.

"None of your business." Then, abashed: "Leave me take care of things. I'll forget something if you don't stop fussing."

A minute later she is humming to herself.

The household has taken on an expectant air, Christmas-like. I find myself putting extra things in my basket for her when I go shopping. Now I ask her if she needs warmer stockings, a new apron, another set of underwear. Her back is to me as she rumbles around in the depths of the oak chest.

"You're not sending me off to school," she says, chiding me gently for hovering. Then she caws and pulls an embroidery hoop from the deepest corner, holding it up like a shiny button stolen from the clothesline. It is unkind but true: every day Godmother turns into more of an old crow. Her crinkly black skirts trail behind her like worn-out feathers, and the skin stretches tighter across her thin, beak-like nose, so tight that the bone shines through, a yellow stain between her eyes.

I should be frightened for her, but her good spirits overwhelm my own good sense.

On Friday morning the children are uneasy and jittery. I have canceled Saturday morning school, and so at first this seems to me the normal high spirits they manage to conjure up at the end of the week. But at recess I understand, finally, how distracted I have been, because the children have managed to plan something behind my back. I truly am surprised when they march, every one of them, toward the house where Godmother sits in her rocking chair. Each of them fishes something out of a pocket to put in her lap: chocolate or hard candy or a piece of fruit.

Two children tarry with Godmother. Laura is talking in a flood of words, her hands moving in the air. Martin stands to one side, his head lowered, nodding once in a while. It is time to end recess, but this sight holds me where I am: the two children, determined and painfully earnest; the old woman, listening carefully, her eyes moving from face to face.

When Laura pauses, Martin picks up. Hanna nods at him with the same kind attentiveness. Finally she reaches out to take them each by the hand. After a while, their shoulders rounded, they leave her.

I would give anything I own to know what she said to them, to hear how she told them goodbye.

By late afternoon, when school is out, there is still no sign of Mikatrin. I know for a fact that she has not yet given up, so I am not surprised when Martin arrives while we are sitting in the *Schopf* folding laundry. He is hauling the small animal cart, and he unloads his best goat and a cage with two laying hens, but he moves slowly. I suspect Mikatrin has sent him to deliver more than just these animals.

When Martin has made the animals to home in my little stable, he comes out to lean against the *Schopf* wall and tap his wooden leg against the lower step. He is nervous and unhappy, and he looks at us with his face all pulled out of shape.

"Don't you fuss at me now, Martin," Godmother murmurs. "You brung me a fine goat, and I appreciate it. I will think of you with kindness while I'm drinking her milk."

"A-yo." He squints up at me, thoughtful. Martin is a good man. Looking at him here, I know he is thinking about Mikatrin waiting for him at home, expecting things from him that he cannot give her. My aggravation with Mikatrin and worry about Godmother give way a little so I can find room to feel sorry for him.

"We'll tell Mikatrin you yelled and hollered for a good while," I suggest. "To no avail."

"None at all," Godmother adds, grinning.

Martin frowns. "This is a serious business, and you two are acting like children."

"You calling me senile, Martin?"

"No ma'am," Martin answers, and he sighs. "You'll tell Mikatrin I made a terrible fuss?"

"For more than an hour," I assure him.

"That leaves us time for a cup of coffee," he says, and comes up on the porch.

While we are sitting over coffee and cake, folks start to arrive. Dairy Olga comes in first. She is Godmother's closest friend since she came to live in the village; they talk about times past, about Olga's grandfather, Bengato Alois, who was a farmer in the old tradition and a great friend of Godmother's. About Olga's brothers, who all fell in the war: Leo, Mikatrin's first husband, in Norway; Tony and Jos in Russia; Jakob in Italy.

Olga puts a knitted blanket in Godmother's lap without a word and is glad to have a cup of coffee with us.

Half-Moon Hollow's Lorenz shows up next, a bottle of his homemade schnapps under his arm, his cap twisted between swollen fingers. On his heels comes Laura.

She is not shy, as most children are who come into my kitchen. Without hesitation she comes forward to put a small package in Godmother's lap. It is wrapped in red paper with a carefully tied white bow, the shape and size of a book. There is a card tucked in the top, in a homemade envelope.

"What's this?" Hanna asks, delighted.

"You shouldn't have a Christmas without any presents up there," Laura says. "Promise you won't open it early?"

"That's a hard promise for her to keep," I tell Laura dryly.

"True enough," Godmother laughs. "Curiosity has always been my downfall."

Laura looks thoughtful at this.

"Maybe a hint would hold her over," Olga offers.

"A-yo," observes Martin. "A hint would be welcome."

"It's about someplace far away," Laura says. "Someplace warm."

"Well, then, something to think about when the January snows start pressing in on you," says Lorenz.

This silences us. We all turn inward to the same picture: Gunta Steeple, lost in snow.

They straggle in one by one, her old friends: Grumpy Marie and Stante from the old folks' home; the priest, who is still a stranger to us all although he has been here since the war; others I haven't seen in a while. Soon the kitchen is full. I make coffee again and again, and put out cookies and cake until everything is gone.

Martin gets up to go and motions me out into the hall.

"About your sister," he scratches his head. "She's scared," he says finally.

"She's mad."

"That too."

We think about this for a while.

"It'll break Godmother's heart if Mikatrin don't give in and come to wish her well," I tell him.

"I'll see what I can do, but you know your sister."

Better than you, I think, but there is no reason to say this. No good reason at all.

That evening Godmother's energy is gone. She sits quietly at the kitchen table watching the fields and mountains fade into darkness.

I am nervous. So nervous that I splash the soup on myself while I am stirring it; so nervous that I dare not think about cutting bread. I am not nervous because Godmother is going away, maybe for good; it is nothing so selfless and graceful as that. I am nervous because I want something from her before she goes. The warmth of my conceit makes me sweat; I feel the moisture break out on my forehead.

If you don't ask her now, you will never know the truth, I tell myself. And then: *Is that such a terrible thing?*

While I am arguing with myself, I ladle soup. Suddenly Godmother speaks without looking at me.

"What's the first thing you recall about the Steeple?"

She has taken me by surprise. Grateful for an excuse to put aside my own thoughts, I consider my answer for a while.

"The time I fell into the burning nettles."

"You were three then, Hans just back from the war. Nothing before that?"

"Nothing comes to mind."

"What about inside? Anything from inside?"

This tone is unusual from Godmother. In a disquieting flash, I remember exactly when it was I last heard it: during the war, across a crackling telephone connection. The day Godmother rode down to Rosenau to use the factory telephone, and waited all day for the call to go through, and then waited again while they found me and brought me to the phone. Her voice, hazy with dread and sorrow, just as it is now, related those things she thought I must know: that Mikatrin's only child, a little girl of four years, had drowned in the well while I was in another land, teaching other people's children how to read and write.

She is waiting for my answer.

"I remember waking up in the morning and seeing the Steeple in the sky like a finger."

But this clearly doesn't satisfy her. She turns toward me in her seat. Her face is all bone; I pull back from its hollows and shadows.

"Do you remember the drawing that hung on the wall?"

"The one of you? The one that disappeared? Only from hearing Mama worry about it, about things being taken from the Steeple."

"All these years I wondered if you'd ever ask me about that picture."

"What about it?"

Hanna shrugs. "Where it came from. Who drew it."

"Who drew it?" I ask numbly.

"Your father drew it the summer you were conceived, right up there at the alp."

"Däta couldn't draw," I respond. Then all at once it comes clear to me, what she has said.

"Däta couldn't draw," I repeat stupidly.

"Your father could draw," she says.

I put the soup on the table and sort out spoons, my fingers wooden and clumsy. Once again I consider cutting the bread, but the overhead light in the kitchen is so bright that the glare on the knife makes me squint. I sit down and look Godmother in the eye.

She reaches across the table, and her fingers, hot and dry, press into my flesh. "You're not surprised. What rumors have you heard?"

Shaking, I pull my wrist away. "No rumors."

"How did you know that Hans weren't your father?"

Finally the words are spoken, and finally I can call up an image: a man with blond hair falling over a bony, sunburned forehead into blue eyes. Not my father.

I gesture toward my face. "Because of my eyes. My hair. He must have been dark. Was he dark?"

She nods. "Angelika lived in fear of it getting out. Of Hans figuring it out."

My throat is very dry. "Godmother. Did I understand you right? My father—was he from the village?"

Her chin jerks up. "No!"

"But he spent that summer at the Steeple?"

She nods.

"He drew a picture of you and he fathered me and then he went away? Mama never saw him again?"

Godmother Johanna's voice rises and wavers. "Angelika never saw him at all."

It takes some time for me to make sense of these words, which slide away from my grasp and refuse to order themselves in my mind.

"I don't understand," I say, although I do. I see the truth on her face. She is all aflush. Her chin trembles, but she holds it up defiantly, as if she expects me to stop her.

I could stop her. I could walk away.

When she is sure I am not going to leave, she says, "In the summer of 1916 I fell in love with a soldier and he gave me you, and when you were born I gave you up to my sister."

Not a word more. She puts this out on the table and it sits there between us; we stare at it.

A picture comes to me: a woman sitting on a stool in the *Stadel* with a piglet between her knees. With her clippers she reaches in to snip out the razor-sharp teeth. The piglet squeals as she lets it go.

Shoo! she laughs. *Go on back to your mama now, if she'll have you.*

I am a dark-eyed child, uneasy in my skin. I ask her, *Don't his mama want him?*

She grabs me and hugs me hard. Her apron smells of the garden where she spends all her free time, of earth and the sun on growing things, the tang of tomato plants.

Of course she wants him, she tells me. *She couldn't live without him.*

"What happened to the soldier?" I ask.

"I don't know for sure," Johanna says. "But you could find out, if you wanted to."

From inside her blouse she takes an envelope, and from inside the envelope a piece of paper about the size of her hand. She puts it on the table and smooths it carefully. This must be the drawing that hung on the wall at the alp and then disappeared the year the war ended. A pencil drawing, soft lines and shadows. A woman, not a young woman, but younger than I am now. Sitting on the ground with her legs off to one side, one hip jutting up under her skirts, the crippled hip, double fists of bone. Her hair is unbraided; it flows over her shoulders and down to the ground in waves. Even in this simple drawing it is full of light and very beautiful.

Hanna reaches out and turns the sheet over. There is a map on the back, of the alp and the mountains around it. It is skillfully done, but she is pointing to something else: a few lines of poetry. Further down, a name written in a strong hand, a hand not her own. Almost against my will, I lean in closer to read what my father wrote on this piece of paper forty-three years ago. A name that means nothing to me. An address in Tirol, or what used to be Tirol and has been Italy since 1919. Another address, in Verona.

"You never wrote."

"No."

"Why not?"

"Because I didn't want to know."

"What?"

Godmother shakes her head.

"Why are you telling me about this now?"

"Because I am a vain old woman," she says. "Because I am selfish."

Late that night, because I am sleepless, Bengato Peter's Jakob comes to me. Jakob fell in the war but he refused to be buried. For sixteen years now he has come to call at odd moments.

Jakob comes to me and reminds me of the day his brother Leo married my sister Mikatrin. He reminds me how we slipped away from the party when the dancing was at its peak, how he drew me, laughing and protesting but wild with schnapps and wanting him, into Hanna's vegetable garden and bedded me among the carrots and potatoes. I remember, now that he reminds me, how the lacy fronds of the carrot tops touched my face as he found his way into me. The rich smell of the earth wrapped around us. I remember the moon, a golden disk punched into the night sky, resting on Jakob's shoulder.

He reminds me, too, as he sometimes does with no bitterness at all, of the men I comforted during the war when I was sent away to teach near the Front. The names and faces come back to me all at once, although I have not thought of many of them for years. Martin's face slides past me and is gone.

When Jakob has left me—it is just past three in the morning—I get up and dress and slip on my shoes and jacket in the dark. There is enough moonlight to show me the way through a world dampened in grays and blues, although I know the route well. It leads out my door and down the lane, over a footbridge and through the church square.

The graveyard gate stands partially open, its wrought-iron mouth swinging silently. On the walkway, gravel gnashes under my shoes.

The morning my mother was to be buried, I volunteered to do the milking and go into the dairy on my own. Leo was frantic with trying to get cut hay under roof before the mourners came to escort Mama away; he was thankful for my help, but too distraught to stop and tell me so. Johanna barely noted my going; she was keeping watch in front of Mama, her rosary tapping at the side of the coffin as the beads slipped away prayer by prayer.

Mikatrin was still in childbed, her tears falling on the face of the little girl who nursed at her breast.

What I hadn't told them when I hitched up the milk cart and hurried off with it was that I had an errand to run, someplace to go on the morning my mother would be buried. I left the horse and cart at the dairy and walked away, and this is where I came, slipping into this very graveyard in the earliest morning to watch the sexton at work, to see where my mother would rest. I stood right here, off to one side where he wouldn't notice me. The early morning sun was already hot, and the back of his neck as brown and tough as saddle leather.

He worked fast, his shovel taking great chunks out of the family grave, which had just recently settled all the way since Daddy was put to rest. In the time I had been away at school, the family had been stopping at the grave every Sunday after mass to pray, and in return, every Sunday the grave had sunk a little bit further into the earth, taking him further away from the living.

The marker is a column as tall as I am. Each of the four sides is full of fine engraving, much of it faded now. Toward the bottom of the front panel there was room for my mother's name. And as the sexton worked, making a place for her body as there was a place for her name, an anger came over me at the unfairness of it, that Mama's name should be there at the bottom, underneath her husband's name and the names of all his kin before him, when her bones were to rest on top of them all. And as I was thinking of this and struggling with it, wishing that land was plentiful enough to give each of us a resting place of our own, wishing that we needn't all crowd together in the end, I heard the shovel strike something solid.

The sexton began to haul forth great shovelfuls of darker earth, loamy and clinging, and with it shards of the last wood coffin that had been resigned to the confined space, and the bones of the man who had occupied it, the man I called my father, and the bones of his people.

The sexton was in the grave to his hips. As he worked, briefly displacing those people from their resting place, pausing to stack larger bones neatly by the edge of the hole, I was struck by the thought that those bones and scraps of clothing had been jumbled through and through by each new burial; every time one of their own came to join them, the dead jostled together not just to make room but to change their view, like children scurrying for good seats at the table, wanting to be close to the cookstove or far away from a father's sharp eye, wanting a chance to look out the window into the bright sun or rain or snow.

And suddenly all my anger was gone. I imagined Mama at that table, a young girl again, surrounded by people who welcomed her and were pleased that she had come.

When I visit the graveyard at night like this, which I sometimes do, it seems to me that I can hear them talking among themselves.

Now, all these years after Mama was put to rest here, I want to talk to her. I want to know if it matters, where I came from, or if one day they will move together and aside and be happy to welcome me as they welcomed her, when it is my turn to join them.

In the end, I can't quite find my voice, but that's all right. I remember that it is my mama there, and in her arms, resting in the cradle of her bones, is Mikatrin's little girl, Maria. Mama knew how to comfort little girls. She whispers to Maria, I am sure, humming the songs she once sang to me, while they wait for the day when the shovel will open the door and the next one of us– maybe Johanna, when the winter is done–will walk through. And then they will all be there, waiting for me, and when I am ready to come to them they will have embraced each other and merged into one woman who is mother and sister and aunt and daughter. And I will not have to choose between them.

I lie down over them, my ear to the earth where I imagine Mama's heart has faded away into the soil. I listen.

On the way back I stop briefly at the schoolhouse, because in the little library I have put together there is an Italian dictionary and grammar. At home at my desk, I work over the poem that my father copied out for Johanna, attributed by him to

Petrarch. By dawn, drawing hard on my school Latin, I have extracted all I can from those few lines of Italian.

Diana never pleased her lover as much
when he saw her naked, bathing in cold waters,
as the simple mountain girl pleases me
when she washes the cloth that binds her hair
so that even in the hot sunlight
she causes me to tremble with the chill of love.

I copy the lines over again, in my best hand, fold the sheet in half and put it in an envelope. Then I find Laura's present, and I carefully unwrap it. When I have slipped my envelope inside for Johanna to find on Christmas Eve, I rewrap the package. I put the drawing back on the kitchen table where she left it.

With the dawn I think of Jakob as I do in the light of day: not of the man who comes to me in the darkness, but of bones scattered somewhere under a white-hot Mediterranean sky, turning to sand. With the dawn I dare to wonder whether my father comes to Johanna in the night.

Sitting at my desk, I hear her moving through the house, getting ready. She makes breakfast as she has done for me every morning for many years now. This thought has not occurred to me before, that I will have to make my own breakfast tomorrow, and the day after. I hear the sound of the farina hitting the hot fat in the old black skillet, the cups being put on the table, the radio turned on.

When she is ready for me, I join my mother for breakfast.

The last homestead we pass is Bengat, where Klaus is watering his geraniums. He raises a hand in greeting, and Johanna raises her cane in return. Caesar turns onto the wide forest path that cuts up and away to the alp. The little cart, well oiled and balanced, turns with him. I glance back from my spot up front to make sure everything is secure: the many treasures too precious to send up in the gondola, the chickens in their cage, Godmother's feather bed, the present in its shiny red paper. The goat ambles along behind on a long lead.

Godmother is perched on the back of the cart, her cane across her lap. When things get steep she will have to walk for a bit, as she can no longer sit Caesar. I am worried about this, but there's nothing to do but try. As we climb, the forest opens its arms now and again to reveal the changing scene below: the village, the church, my little house. From here we can't see Bent Elbow, but that will come in time.

Godmother squawks. I stumble a little as I turn around in surprise. I see what she sees, on a bit of rolling pastureland far below us: a woman moving in long strides up toward the path. She is half an hour behind us. Mikatrin.

"Should we wait?"

"No!" Godmother says, waving me on. "She'll catch up."

"Caesar could use the rest," I say as I smooth my skirt and settle next to her on the edge of the cart. "Tell me a story."

"Haven't you had enough stories for a while?" But she smiles as she says this, and then looks around as if waking from a long sleep. "I wonder how many times I been up and down this way."

"Tell me about a time you remember."

"April 1917," she says. "I talked your mama into going up to the alp early to check over the place. We got Goat-Cheese Willi's Klaus to look after the livestock at the homestead, just for two nights. The weather was fine, and I was big with child and tired of hiding from folks. I just wanted to be up at the Steeple. Guess I was hoping your father might come back.

"We woke up the first night in a snowstorm, took us by surprise. There was food for a few days, but Angelika was wor-

Lilimarlene

Bengat Homestead 1974

When Lilimarlene handed in her letter of resignation and explained that she was leaving the province hospital to move home to Rosenau, the director of nursing looked her up and down, not in anger, but with a kind of puzzlement. She said, "You are throwing away a brilliant career." And: "What are you thinking?"

That look of reluctant admiration often came back to Lili as she puttered on her scooter up one mountainside and down another, from home visit to home visit. *I had a brilliant career,* she sometimes murmured to herself when the weather was particularly bad or when her patient smelled worse than anything piled outside his barn. *In a warm, clean hospital.*

But the mornings were good. She had forgotten what it was like to be outside in the daytime, what the light could do to the mountains, what the air smelled like up here. Every evening Dr. Troy gave her a list for the next morning, and Lili went off ried about having to deliver you. She was scared to the quick, not knowing what to do if something went wrong." Godmother paused.

"Of course, I didn't pay her much mind. I didn't think you'd come along until the end of the month. But then the next day, it was at three in the afternoon, my water broke. Angelika was right torn, should she say she told me so, or just sit right down and die of fright. And Mikatrin. Poor child, never knowing what was coming her way.

"There was a wood sledge in the *Stadel*. Soon as the snow let up, we drug it out and we wrapped ourselves up with all the blankets and featherbeds we had. Angelika wiped the tears off her face and hitched up Nero and tied me and Mikatrin to the flatbed with a length of rope, and we were off for Bengat. Angelika was nervous about those steep stretches, about us breaking away and ending up over a cliff, but I knew that Nero would get us down safe. What I didn't know was how it would be to hand you over to Angelika. How hard that would be."

She takes my hand in her own.

"I have dreamed of that sled ride many times since. This forest was silent as sleep, except for Nero's hooves and the rush of the runners through the snow. Everything white on white, the trees all tangled with ice, all shot with color in the last of the sun. The village below us, lamplights coming up one by one, scattered here and there. Then the moon rising full, burning red, the sky darker and darker. The child in me moving down, the pain starting slow in waves. Mikatrin leaning back against me, needing my comfort."

Godmother stops. Mikatrin is coming toward us on the path. A maple leaf, bright scarlet, is caught in her hair. A grown woman, her face set in willfulness and sorrow and fear.

"That's the last story I've got to tell," Godmother says, and she puts her other hand out toward my sister.

at daybreak to change dressings, look into sore ears, check umbilical cords, take out stitches.

People were glad to see her when she showed up at the door. Old folks especially, who tried to keep her as long as they could with their troubles and their stories and their finagling for whatever gossip might be had. They called her "Alois's oldest" and "poor little lamb," sent her away with sweets in her pockets as if she were still a schoolgirl and not the rightful employee of the villages of Ackenau and Rosenau, the visiting nurse. But still everybody wanted to know why she had come home.

She could see it in the younger ones, girls who were too much in awe of her to ask any question straight out; they smiled at her from the corner as she listened to the wheezy chests of little brothers. Their older sisters, women Lili's age with two or three children, were too busy in kitchen and cowshed and hay-field to be envious, too sure of their husbands to be jealous. But they wondered too. "Look who the breeze blew in," they would say when she came by to check a sprain or take a temperature. "Never thought we'd see you around here anymore."

The old folks were more direct. On a June morning soon after Lili moved back home, as she stood on the church square contemplating the new ADEG store that had been built on the spot where her grandfather's homestead stood until it burned down, Pitchfork Gottfried climbed off his tractor to talk to her. "*Jesus nah*," he cried, pumping her hand. "So here you are!" Then he nodded toward the ADEG. White stucco and plate glass, sad-looking cabbage and green-tinged peaches from Italy in the bins out front.

"Folks can say what they want about the Wainwright," Gottfried said, "but his old place suited us rough ones better. Your mama was born and raised right there. You remember the Wainwright?"

"He died before I was born."

"Course he did," said Gottfried. He cleared his throat and

grinned at her. "So what are you doing back here, girlie? You looking for a sweetheart?"

It was a popular theory: she had given up her career because she couldn't find a man, or had lost some exotic flat-lander to a city woman who wore too much makeup. Lili was more than ready to breed, after all, at twenty-seven.

"Naturally, Gottfried," Lili said. "Now if only you were available, things would be a lot easier."

"Oh, you won't get the likes of me," he laughed. "A farmer don't need an over-smart wife. An educated girl like you wouldn't know what to do with a farmer."

Lili knew this wasn't true, but it stung anyway.

"Well, what kind of sweetheart did you have in mind for me," she asked him.

He shrugged. "Asked if you was looking. Never said you'd find one."

When there was too little time between her last home visit and her shift at the old folks' home to go back to Bengat, Lili ate her noonday meal at the Eagle. The innkeeper's wife had taken Lilimarlene on as a project, and she served her suggestions with every course. Today it was the church choir, which could always use another alto to stand up to those pushy sopranos; and by the way, Hedwig wanted to know, could Lili have a look at the cat? Folks might be distrustful of her many years away, but they had a healthy respect for her education and medical training; anyway, she was cheaper than the vet.

The tom had been out for days and had come home to roll himself into a pitiful bundle under the bar, oblivious to the shuffling of heavy clogs around him. Lili pulled him out and ran a hand over his head. He trilled a tired hello and curled into her arms, displaying a well-chewed ear and a fresh battle wound above one eye; he was all bone and sinew.

The farmers put down their liters of Ackenauerbräu to evaluate her bedside manner.

"Nothing wrong with him that food won't fix," said Cobbler's Sefftone.

Tanna Hanso Tonile grinned. "He's just been on the prowl, Hedwig."

"Running his own flesh to rack and ruin for a bit of the other," said Kasparle's Jos, but he wasn't looking at the tomcat. Lili felt his eyes on her.

Suddenly she got a clear picture of Jos as a boy. They had been in school together; he learned to read late, but he could do sums in his head faster than Miss Martha, and he had an uncommon way with the spoken word. He wrote dialect poetry and had always taken some teasing for that. There was a poem in the paper now and then, so he hadn't given it up.

"A-yo," agreed Lilimarlene, handing the tom over to Hedwig. "He's only doing what instinct drives him to do."

Jos was the last one to let her gaze go. Lili went back to her dinner knowing that the farmers watched her, that they could not help measuring the span of her hips and the depth of her chest, wondering what instincts she might have and where they drove her.

Afternoon duty at the old folks' home was the harder part of her day. There were five permanent residents: the old sexton, who had lost both his legs below the knees to diabetes; Bent Elbow's Johanna, who at ninety-four slept most of the day and daydreamed the rest away, but needed a lot of care; Gide's Hannes, the last of the veterans from the First War, addled beyond repair; and Wainwright's Stante and Grumpy Marie, both related to Lili by blood. Sister Peter Josef and Sister Maria Theres kept them clean, fed them properly, read to them, prayed with them, but they needed nursing too. All except Stante.

Seventy-three years old, and still he was in a state of health that put many younger men to shame.

Stante could have lived at Bengat, where Lili's uncles Christian and Klaus would gladly have taken him in for the company and his monumental endurance in the hayfield. But he was devoted to Grumpy Marie and he wouldn't leave her. Marie had outlived everyone who might have been persuaded to take her in, and so she and Stante lived at the home, his sweet temperament never quite outweighing the ongoing burden of her sour humor and bad manners.

It had occurred to Lili that Marie was one of the reasons Dr. Troy had been so persistent in asking her to come home to nurse. The others had their bad days, but they also had family who came in regularly to help out; Marie was dependent on the nuns alone, but she didn't hesitate to test their goodwill to the breaking point. Dr. Troy pointed out to Lili that Marie needed somebody bound to put up with her by the double knot of professional obligation and blood tie, and she knew that this was true.

"Time for your medicine," Lili said to Marie first thing, having learned that pleasantries worked no magic at all and sometimes made matters worse.

"That's your mother's job," snapped Marie without turning away from the window. Her hands clung to the arms of her wheelchair like roots forced up by the frost, nails ridged yellow, joints swollen. But her heartbeat was strong and her will to live even stronger; Lili could well imagine that just five years from now the village would pull itself together to celebrate her hundredth birthday, put her up in a horse-drawn carriage decorated with garlands and drive her around the church square like a Relic of the Cross. Right now, though, her mind was wandering.

"My mother's dead," Lili said patiently, and went to fill the water carafe.

Marie's voice wobbled after her. "Who told you that!" she cried. "Such foolishness!"

Lili laid out the spoon and measured medication and folded the towel while Marie eyed her suspiciously. She was near blind now, but her ears were sharp.

"What's that?"

"Your medicine," said Lili. "For your circulation."

"Don't want it."

"But you do need it."

"Let Katharina give it to me."

"My mother's dead," said Lili once again. "You remember. The coach that rolled over on the Ackenau road. The snowslide." She heard Stante shuffling behind her; he grunted.

"Nineteen hundred and fifty," he said clearly.

"She is my half sister," said Marie, ignoring him. "We both had the Wainwright for our daddy. I would know if she was dead." She pursed her lips. "She would come and tell me so. If she's dead, why don't she come tell me so?"

"Open up now," Lili murmured.

Marie wiggled her eyebrows and shut her lips tight.

Holding the spoon in her right hand, Lili stroked one finger down Marie's cheek. "You need this medicine."

"I need your mother," Marie corrected, and Lili slipped the spoon in.

In the half hour before Lili left for home, she made it her habit to sit with Marie. If she had any good time at all it was in the fading light of the summer evening, so when Lili had finished with the old sexton she came in.

Marie started up right away. "You don't believe in ghosts."

"You know I don't," Lili said.

"They are all around. Go next door, ask Johanna. She's got a regular crew comes to visit her. It's even more crowded since the cancer took Martha. Sometimes I wonder where Mikatrin will find a place to sit when she comes to call."

"I have never seen a ghost," said Lili.

"So much for education," snorted Marie. "Have you ever seen God? You believe in him, don't you?"

Lili got up to adjust the curtains.

"Ask your uncle Klaus," Marie suggested. "Ask him about Jakob." After a time, she sighed. "What was your mama doing on that coach, anyway?" The evening light lay in puddles on her lap, where her fingers twitched and worked the wool of her shawl.

"I don't know," said Lilimarlene. "We'll never know."

Marie sat still, her eyes darting back and forth as if watching a conversation between two people long gone. "Your mama meant well, and don't let people tell you otherwise. She left you well provided for. Hasn't Alois always treated you like his own? Of course he has."

It was a question people always asked of Lili and then answered for her.

"I'll tell you something, something most folks won't dare admit," Marie said, her head trembling. "Sometimes no mother a-tall is better than the one you get dealt. Your granny Theres was the biggest part of your mama's problem. Do you remember her?"

Lili shook her head.

"Good." Marie nodded. "Good. Best to forget her."

Suddenly Marie leaned forward in the chair and took Lili's wrist, her cold grip as unforgiving as ice. "Why'd you come back here?"

"I'm trying to figure that out myself," Lili said. It was as close to the truth as she could get.

Lili had had a choice: she could have moved back into the *Sennhaus*, where her father still lived with her stepmother. It was Lili's home, after all: she still called them Däta and Mama. She had lived with them above the dairy until Miss Martha talked Alois into sending her to school out in the valley. Folks called her Dairy Lili still, although she had only been there for holidays and weekends all these years.

But she had been living in the nurses' residence for too long and had had enough of the company of women; when the uncles offered her a home at Bengat, she was glad to accept. They gave her the *Gada*, the big bedroom that looked out on the Praying Hands, and she slept in the bed where her grandmother Olga was born. After just a few weeks, Lili knew she had done the right thing. She was glad to be out of the village, in spite of the bad road, in spite of the fact that Bengat was the only homestead in Rosenau still without an indoor toilet. "You'll change your mind one night in January sitting in that outhouse," her father had said to her, but without any malice at all. Lili thought he didn't really mind: her three half sisters were still at home, and Alois could do without a fifth female, as long as Lili was close enough for him to see most days.

The uncles had been pleased to get her, hoping to draw her into their arguments and Saturday night *Jass* games. They were bachelor farmers, not especially good at it, but they cut enough hay to overwinter their few animals, got enough milk to the dairy to bring in a little cash. Christian made some extra money mending whatever leather goods folks brought by. Since Grandma Olga died Klaus had cooked and taken care of the house. He spent the rest of his time looking after his cats and his garden and flower boxes, petunias and geraniums of the most garish shades, purples and reds and oranges all jumbled together. The uncles were young yet, Klaus less than forty, but their eccentricities—long flowing beards and ice baths every morning at 4:30—were enough to scare off any prospective bride.

At table that evening Lili turned to Klaus. "Grumpy Marie says to ask you about ghosts. About Jakob."

Christian grunted into his coffee cup.

Klaus told her about his uncle Jakob, who had died in the last war but found his way home to pay visits to certain people. Klaus had seen him twice: once when he was a boy, right after the war, and once just before his mother–Lili's grandmother–died.

"Granny Olga? Did she see him too?"

"A-yo. She saw him. Right before she took her heart attack. He was standing at the window. She was disappointed he didn't bring Daddy along with him to fetch her."

"Does he still come around?" Lili asked.

Klaus shrugged. "Haven't heard much about him lately. Maybe he don't care to come anymore, since Miss Martha passed away. Some say they were sweethearts."

Christian snorted. "Some say a lot of things."

"Have Granny or Miss Martha ever come to call?" Lili asked.

Klaus gave her a long, hard look. "They were ready to pass over," he said patiently, as if she must be embarrassed not to understand something so obvious. "Jakob wasn't."

Lili watched Christian pour more milk into his coffee cup. The flimsy skin that floated on top of the hot milk slipped over the jug's rim, and he caught it with his spoon, brought it to his mouth.

"You're wondering if your mama ever comes around," he said finally, not looking at Lili. Christian had a mean streak sometimes, and he could be hard, but he was also quicker than Klaus and not afraid to say what he saw plainly.

"Have you ever seen my mama's ghost?" she asked then, her voice cracking.

"No," said Klaus, answering for Christian. "I guess she never felt the need to wander."

That night Lili went with the uncles to the *Kilbe* dance, a celebration that was supposed to mark the anniversary of the church's founding, but over the years had become more of a midsummer festival. Christian and Klaus argued for such a long time about whether to take the tractor or the scooters or walk that she finally set off without them. Eventually they caught up with her, and she stood on the back of the tractor holding her skirt up and away, letting the warm evening breeze touch her face. They got to the Eagle late, but there were still men outside. Lili saw the eyes turn to watch her, she saw their approval and wariness; they prowled the church square, their gaze skittering back to her again and again as she walked up the steps.

Stante was standing just inside the door. If there was something going on at the Eagle, Stante was always there. While Grumpy Marie slept, he made himself known at wedding parties, *Fasching* dances, meetings of the Hog Breeders Local or the village council, *Jass* competitions, *Heimatabend* for the tourists. He could not stay away, and nobody minded him; brides threw him kisses, and their grooms made sure Stante's beer glass was full. He never danced, he never got drunk; sometimes he helped others get home who weren't so moderate in their pursuits. Now Stante grinned at Lili and shuffled forward to grasp her hand in both of his. "Pretty," he said, "pretty."

The dancing was under way, the room filled with smoke and loud talk. The musicians were up on the stage in red vests and lederhosen, brass instruments flashing in the lights. A double-step polka started, and she let Klaus pull her out onto the dance floor; when the set of three was done she danced with Christian and then with her father.

Throughout the whole first dance he was silent except to ask her could she come by tomorrow, Nini had a bad cold, maybe the influenza. Alois had a deep, gruff voice that he didn't use very much, but his children never doubted his affection. While Lili was away at school and then at work, he wrote her a postcard every week, always the same postcard, of the Rosenau church square in the fall. She had kept every one of them, hundreds of them.

"Do you ever see any ghosts?" she asked him suddenly, and felt his arms jerk.

"Grumpy Marie was talking today about ghosts," she said lamely.

"Ghosts run in the family," he said at last. "We don't have to go looking for them."

But I do, Lili wanted to say to him. *It seems that I do.*

She danced with anybody who asked her; it was the thing to do. Some of them made her laugh; others questioned her about cures for backache or told her about their geese or goats or prize hogs or motorcycles; a few wanted her opinion on politics or dehorning cows or whether or not it was just an old superstition that cutting your hair on the waning moon made it fall out.

Lili liked the dancing, the shuffle-step polkas and the double-step ones that everybody called "stumbling" but not many men could do well. The fastest dances sent the room spinning, circles within circles. She waited for the high hooting yodel in three notes that the men let wing through the room when the dance was at its peak. Moving on the balls of her feet, then dancing hard and putting her heels down. The glass in the window frames shimmying with the rhythmic stamping of heavy shoes. Letting a man lead with no apologies, the muscles of his upper arm hard under her left hand, the shifting pressure of his palms enough to tell her what she needed to know, how to move. The waltzes, with their deep sweeps, right around, left around.

Between dances she sat with her stepmother and her father and drank Ackenauerbräu. The uncles had disappeared into the crowd of bachelors who hung in a pack near the door.

Men whose names she hardly recalled came to claim

her. The floor was crowded now; people had been drinking, and footwork suffered. A tall man from Nenau in a red-checked shirt, his dialect telling a tale on him, propelled her through the crowd. "Don't know your face," he said to her, "but you sure can move." An elbow intruded between them. He swore. "People will get rowdy just when I find a good dancer."

Bent Elbow's Rudi at her back, wanting her to dance. She wondered if he remembered the time he kissed her, in the basement of the school; she must have been nine, he was a year younger. He had always been big for his age. Hands like boards, crooked teeth but white and clean. A headful of red curls falling into his eyes.

"You look like Martin," she told him, meaning his older brother.

"But I dance better than him."

"You're more humble, too," she laughed.

"Martin married his Laura," said Rudi. "Stick with me."

Lili thought he would start to talk, to tell her about the new house he had built for himself, about his business. But he was content to dance. Finally she asked him about that kiss, knowing that it was the beer asking.

"That wasn't me," Rudi said. "But we could arrange some kissing, if you've got the mind."

"Of course it was you," Lili said.

"Must have been dark in that cellar if you couldn't tell the difference between me and Kasparle's Jos."

She startled. "How would you know that?"

"Everybody knows about that, Lilimarlene. Jos always had an eye for you. Look at him over there, he's been watching you all night."

She felt the truth of this prickle on the back of her neck. "A man who won't dance with me hardly seems like somebody who would have kissed me in the school cellar," she said, and Rudi put back his head and laughed.

Then the set was done, and he took her by the elbow and led her to her seat beside her father.

Rudi headed straight for Jos. Lili's face burned. A strumming in her hands, her fingers dancing on her lap. What to do. A grin wanted to show itself; Lili pushed it away impatiently. Tomorrow it would be all over the village. Numb, she watched Jos start across the room toward her, saw the set of his jaw; too late to escape. Not that she wanted to, she told herself. Not that she couldn't handle this.

Jostled against him on the dance floor, Lili tried not to look at his face, and then she found out the truth: he was the best dancer she had ever known. She wondered if she should compliment him. If he would get more of the wrong idea.

"Rudi is right, you know," he said finally. "That was me down there in the cellar. I did it on a dare."

She had to laugh. "I don't believe you," she said.

"Why would I lie about it?"

"Now you are going to tell me I broke your heart when I went away to school."

"No, I'm not going to tell you that at all."

She tried to concentrate on the dancing. Her right hand in his left one; scars on his palm, clean nails. She held her back straight and danced with her feet and legs, following his lead, fast and faster, his footwork steady but with a little twist on the third count that set him apart. His color high, his mouth set firm. The plateau of his shoulders broad and straight, a topline like a good bull's, she thought, surprised and uneasy that this farming term came to her unbidden.

Lili wondered if she should say she had seen his poems in the paper. *No, I'm not going to tell you that at all.*

She concentrated on the hollow at the base of his throat, the sheen of sweat there. Felt her hair swinging around her head. Felt him watching her.

The set ended and she started to walk away; he caught

her hand and pulled her up short, keeping her next to him.

The dance floor was emptier now, and there was space to dance a triple-step. The room swept by in a whirl of sound. Lili wondered if they would ever speak again, or if they would walk past each other forever with just a nod and a regret. Another waltz. They circled the room, past a bank of windows. Hedwig's tomcat poised there, ready to leap out into the night.

"A-yo," Jos said. "Look at him. At it again."

Lili laughed.

"That's better," he said.

"What's better?"

"You're not so stiff."

"What do I have to be stiff about?"

Jos looked at her, his gaze calm. Blue eyes, she thought. *I forgot about his blue eyes.*

181

"The one who claims you for the last dance walks you home," he said. "In case you forgot how it works."

"Is this the last dance?"

"It is."

"What if nobody claims you?"

"Then you walk home with your folks."

"What if you don't want to walk home with the one who claims you?"

"Then you walk home with your folks."

Lili hesitated. "It's a long walk."

"You sound like a city girl. Give us time to talk."

About what? she wanted to say, but then thought better of it. "People will gossip," she said.

"They'll do that anyway."

Lili looked around for her father and stepmother and saw they were gone. The uncles had left, too.

"They went on ahead some time ago," Jos said, reading her mind. "I'll wager they left the porch light on."

* * *

But her folks hadn't all gone home; Stante was waiting on the step with his cap in his hands. He set off with them toward Bengat. Lili wondered if he thought he had to protect her. She looked at Jos, looked away when he caught her gaze.

The sky was cloudless and clear, stars scattered, the night deep and silent. They walked on opposite sides of the road, Lili with her arms wound around herself, Stante in the middle between them. Lili looked up at the stars, at the shapes of the mountains, at silent homesteads: anything but Jos.

She wondered if she should say something to Stante, send him back in the other direction, send him home.

"So did you get down to the soccer game on Sunday?" Jos asked, and Lili was confused until she realized that it was Stante he was talking to.

"A-yo," Stante nodded. "Markus got two goals," he said. "Shoulda seen it."

Lili stumbled. She couldn't remember ever hearing such a long sentence out of Stante. In growing amazement she listened as they talked, Jos about whatever came into his head, Stante sometimes responding, sometimes silent. She realized with a shock that Stante had not come along to look out after her but to talk to Jos. In the night, Stante was just an old man of few words. Lili was ashamed that she had never imagined this.

They came to the Low Road bridge, and Stante stopped suddenly. He looked around as if he was surprised to find himself outside so late. "Better go home," he said. He tilted back his head and looked up at the sky.

"The stars move, if you watch them long enough." Stante turned to Jos. "You'll see her up to Bengat?" he asked, nodding toward Lili. Then he shook their hands. Lili's he held for a little longer, looking at her thoughtfully.

They watched him from the bridge.

"I had no idea," Lili said when he was out of earshot.

"What?"

"That Stante could talk. Like that. Sentences."

"He'll tell you whole stories, if you ask him."

"You are probably the only one who thinks to ask him," Lili said, forgetting not to look at Jos, seeing the way his hair touched his collar, the plane of his cheek.

"He remembers things from the first war that most people never noticed even when they happened," Jos said. "He'll tell you what they did to him when they took him away, if you ask and you can bear to listen."

"Does he ever mention my mother to you?"

"I never asked him. You could."

Lili nodded. "I will," she said.

They stood listening to the night. Around them the smooth lake of pasture dipped and rose, a quilt of silver and shadow; the moon hung very low and full in the sky. They sat down on the edge of the bridge with their feet swinging just above the water.

Off in the distance, Bengat perched up above them.

"It doesn't feel like home," she said, mostly to herself; and was stunned by this, the truth.

Lili let herself be turned toward Jos; she tried to remember the last time she had kissed anybody. Had wanted to kiss anybody. She felt his hands on her face, his mouth, the kiss like a welcoming. As if she hadn't been able to see him until he touched her like this, until she tasted his skin. Peeling him open like a peach, swimming in the pleasure of his kiss.

"Lilimarlene," he whispered against her mouth. "It is, it is home. It is your home."

"Aren't you going to ask me why I came back?" She knew that she was handing him something, a chance, an opening.

"You don't need a reason to come home," Jos said. "You need a reason to stay away."

She asked him. She said, "Do you believe in ghosts?"

Jos shrugged, his fingers moving on her shoulders. "Don't see any reason not to."

"I'd like to believe in them," said Lilimarlene. "But I can't see how." She looked up into the still and unmoving stars, and because she did not know the words to use to summon her mother's ghost, Lili called forth the only memory she had of her. She saw her mother walking away from the house with a cream jug clutched in one hand, her shoulders rolled in against the cold, her head bowed. Twenty-six years old, as old as she would ever get.

How strange, Lili thought, but she didn't trust Jos enough to say it aloud, not yet: how strange some folks won't rest quiet in their graves and others can turn their backs on the living.

Laura

Bent Elbow Homestead 1977

On the day Bent Elbow's Martin's Laura, once known as Kasparle's Laura, started the sixth month of her fourth pregnancy, two things happened: she stopped thinking all the time about the last baby, the lost one, and her wedding ring broke.

It was early evening when she took the children to pick up the milk cans from the stand at the side of the road, Annile scooting ahead down the narrow scythe of path that cut through the hayfields. Laura shifted Jakob on her hip and trudged after her daughter: her muscles twitched and her neck was slick with sweat, her hair heavy and damp under a kerchief shot through with hay dust. Once at the stand, she was glad to load the boy, heavy as he was, into the cart with the empty canisters.

They began to work their way back up the hill to the cowshed. Annile and Laura pushed steadily, heads bowed close together over the cart, bare feet splayed against the warmth of the road. At the top, where the path leveled out, Annile insisted that she could do it herself, so Laura stepped away, trying not to hover.

Annile leaned into the task, her small brown face screwed down upon itself in concentration, and in one good shove the cart tipped smartly sideways.

Laura reached in quick to right it before Jakob could tumble out; stepping back, she felt an odd sharpness against her palm. She looked down and there it was: her wedding ring broken in two against an angry red welt on her finger. And she remembered the first summer they were married, how this very ring had flashed in the sunlight as it rose and fell with the rhythm of the hay rake. Now she put it in her pocket, dull and thin and rent beyond repair.

"Moved it pretty far that time," Laura said to Annile. "Run on now and get the cows in, your daddy's almost ready to start milking."

Then she paused to look westward at the sky, wanting rain, thinking of how much housework she could get done on a cool, wet day with no fieldwork, thinking of a trip to town and of the watchmaker's little collection of rings. But on the western horizon, where the mountains gave reluctant way to the Rhine and the Rhine fed into the warm water of Lake Constance, Laura saw deep blues seeping away into shades of rose. She reconciled herself to another afternoon in the hayfield.

Her mother-in-law would come to hay. She would bring the brothers with her. She would wield her rake like a sword, a dour slip of a woman moving in fits and starts among the five silent men who sailed through the field with great, generous motions. She would set them working faster with a sigh, a nod, a lifted eyebrow. All afternoon she would work like a demon beside Laura and never say a word, but when they were done she would stay behind to talk. She would stand in the middle of the kitchen and she would tell Laura about what was going on in the village, about the dinner she had cooked the pastor, her eyes darting here and there constantly: fly-specked window-panes, weeds in the garden, dust in the corners, runny noses, gray diapers.

A bare ring finger.

"You'll see," Mikatrin had said to her before the wedding as she was moving out and Laura was moving in. "You'll see how this place wears things down."

Martin had brought Laura home on a rainy Sunday and said it straight out in the crowded kitchen where his younger brothers hunched over pork roast and dumplings, cabbage, apple salad, fresh tomatoes: they wanted to get married. The brothers turned to Laura, and she held up her head and met their looks, eye for eye. Rudi was the first to look away; the others dropped their heads too.

Then Mikatrin took Laura to see the third-floor apartment.

"A home inside a home," Mikatrin said as they looked through the two rooms and a bath.

"Snug," she added when they stood on the little balcony under the eaves where two lawn chairs had been set up cheek to jowl.

Mikatrin had made up the apartment for the tourists who wandered over the border from Germany for long weekends: dried flowers in a vase and a sheet of plastic over the red-checked tablecloth. Green flowered curtains with cows on the hem, a cookstove with two electric rings.

"You'll eat with us," Mikatrin went on, flapping her hand-kerchief at a bit of dust on the dresser.

Laura looked out the window over the vegetable garden and the herd grazing on the wet slope of the mountain. Now she understood how things were ordered in this family: patched shoes but triple-A fodder; five brothers in one room, but an apartment for the tourists.

Mikatrin turned away from Laura and licked her finger

to rub it against a fleck in the linoleum counter top. "Martin's father was a good farmer," she told Laura. "A hard worker."

Later, Laura drew on something hard and strong in herself and turned down the arrangement: she understood that there would be no sharing this household with her mother-in-law, that when she looked at herself in the mirror Mikatrin had hung in the little bathroom, she would see a woman who was becoming, day by day, more of a daughter and less of a wife.

"Times you'll wonder why," was all Mikatrin said when Laura made her position known.

To her son, Mikatrin had more to say. But in the end Martin wanted Laura more than he needed to please his mother, and so they waited. They waited two years until each of the brothers had learned a trade: the twins went to apprentice with the cabinetmaker in Ackenau; Rudi built a shop where he could sell radios and tape players, mixers and electric meat slicers; Jok learned how to fix them. All four of them moved with Mikatrin into the little house that she had inherited from Miss Martha. Mikatrin learned to sleep late in the mornings and waited on customers in Rudi's shop when the mood took her, when she wasn't busy in her garden or tending the family graves. Mostly she made it her business to stay away from Bent Elbow, but when the haying was more than Martin and Laura could handle, she would gather the boys together and come for an afternoon.

The third-floor apartment was empty now; sometimes they rented it to skiers when the snow was good.

Laura had got what she wanted.

Now Laura watched her daughter sprint toward the grazing cows, whooping her own call to them, scolding in a high voice: "Hi-ya, hi-ya, mind now! hi-ya!"

The baby laughed, his hands fluttering around his face, and Laura laughed with him, hefting him out of the cart to set him down among the chickens while she carried the milk cans to the barn door. Martin came out to meet her, still pulling himself into his milking gear. Together they watched Jakob crawl after a banty hen.

"Do you think he'll walk before the next one gets here?" he asked, leaning down over her shoulder to chafe her cheek with his stubble.

"Maybe," Laura answered. She put her hand with its red welt against his cheek.

"Look," she said finally.

He took her hand and turned it palm up. "Ma went through four rings, I think it was, before she stopped wearing them altogether," he said.

Jakob squawked suddenly and Laura ran to scoop him up, and in that time Martin disappeared into the cowshed. She put the baby to her hip again and headed for the house.

"Laura!" Martin called after her, leaning out from the doorway.

She stopped, her fingers working the sharp edges of the ring in her apron pocket.

"Do you have time to look in on the sow?"

She nodded, feeling tears tangle in her eyelashes. Now what did you expect, she asked herself. Just what did you expect of him?

The pigpen was large because the sow was large, and growing larger: that was her function, to grow and to produce the piglets that brought so much trouble and profit. There were two boxes, her big one with its trough and a smaller one with a warming lamp, connected by a sliding door that would only be opened at scheduled intervals to let the piglets in to suckle; they were not left in the large pen until they were old enough and smart enough to get out of the sow's way. Even so, one of them would get caught now and then and would have to be hauled out, limp and cold, from under the sleepy sow. If there seemed to be some spark left, the piglet would be put under the warming lamp to recover, because as Mikatrin liked to point out, pigs were tough animals and could stand a lot.

Laura leaned over the rail to have a closer look. The pen was quiet, removed from the constantly shifting weight of the cows, the nervous skittering of the calves: the sow at the height of her term was the heavy heart of the barn. She rested uneasily, grumbling softly when Laura rubbed a hand over the small bright eyes. The animal could go into labor any time; tonight Laura would alternate between bed and barn, relieving Martin every few hours to keep watch.

In the front hall the wildflowers she had arranged so carefully in a pottery vase on the oak chest were drooping, shedding petals in a lazy arc over the floor. Laura watched them fall, then turned and went into the kitchen, warm in the late afternoon sun and buzzing with flies. There were piles of dishes on the washboard, toys scattered everywhere, a basket of ironing and another of mending. From the open window came the sounds of sheets snapping in the breeze and a soft, full thud as a pear fell to the ground.

A little more of the brightness went out of her.

"Come on," she said suddenly to Annile, who watched from the door. "There's more than an hour of sun left, we're going for a walk." She settled Jakob more firmly on her hip and took his sun hat from the peg on the wall.

They played hooky, hurrying up the old stone path that led through the homestead pasture, then into the woods and up to Hutla Meadow and beyond to the rough cliffs of the Praying Hands.

"Can I help when the piglets come, Mama?"

"A-yo," Laura said slowly. "If they come in the daylight."

On a cold March morning the old sow had started to

farrow her last litter before sunrise. Annile had been put on duty fresh out of bed; Laura went out with her to see her settled into the pen. The sow shifted and growled, and a shiny packet slid out: the piglet in its birth sac. It was an early one and strong; it fought its way out on its own. Those to come after might not be so keen: when one appeared, Annile was to yell for her father and Martin would come leaping over animals and milking stools to peel the sac away. Laura showed Annile how to lift the sow's tail to check for progress, and then she went back to the kitchen and her baking.

When they came in to breakfast together, Martin was carrying a cold, limp piglet. The oven had cooled down some, and Laura put him on a tray and slid him in. They might have forgotten him if he hadn't started squealing as they sat down to breakfast. Martin took him back to the litter fully recovered.

"How'd that happen?" Laura asked him when he returned to the table.

"Just one of those things." He never even looked at the child hanging her head over her milk cup.

Laura saw this. She imagined Annile asleep in the warm, steamy stall: the windows streaky with the moisture of animal respiration; the heavy, sweet smells of hay and dung and hot milk thick in the air; Annile's head propped against the wall of the pigpen; Annile lulled away to sleep by the rhythmic rush of milk onto metal. Getting up to fill the jug from the bucket Martin had brought in that morning, Laura paused to run her hand through his hair.

She was thinking about this, about the feel of Martin's hair, when they came to a wire fence. Laura lifted it so that the child could shimmy under, stepping over it herself. The ground grew marshy, and then there was a spring.

They settled themselves on a log propped across the small expanse of water, and Laura eased her swollen feet in, hiccuping at the shock and trying to balance the struggling baby on her lap. He fussed at her until she set him down on the bank. Working his bottom and fists into the mud, he rewarded her with a smile and a grunt.

"Look at the mess," Annile complained. "Old muddy-butt Jakob."

"What d'you want him, muddy or cranky?"

Annile shrugged.

Laura reached down into the spring to let a tadpole slip into her palms; she felt the tentative life shivering there as she had once felt these children who were now irreversibly, inexplicably distinct from her tremble within her; as she felt life there now, strong and growing stronger every day.

With both the children labor had come down hard on her while Martin rushed to finish the morning milking. With Jakob things had moved too fast, and she had waited for Martin bent double to keep herself from pushing. Then they raced all the way to the midwife, Martin pressing the old car into an arthritic and reluctant gallop, slowing down only once as they drove through the church square to yell out the window to Rudi, who was sweeping the walk in front of his shop, that he should send Mikatrin out to Bent Elbow, where they had left Annile asleep in her crib and the cows impatient to get to pasture.

And when they got to Ackenau and the midwife's, Laura hadn't been able to get out of the car. Martin had seen how it was with her and leaned in to snatch her up. Taking the steps two at a time, never breathing hard, he put her down gently as he stepped across the doorsill, where she bent into a bow just in time to catch the child herself, hot and wet and reeking of the womb. The midwife had stood there with her hands outspread, torn between distress and irritation.

It had put a scare into both of them; at the time, Laura couldn't imagine ever being so scared again. Then, the following winter, she woke in the middle of the night, the bedclothes sticky with her own blood, and she learned better. The day she got home from the hospital with the picture of her fragile, pale curl of a baby still burning in her mind, Mikatrin had been waiting.

"I lost my first when she was four," she reminded Laura. "Lost two more after that, both early, like yours." She busied herself folding towels.

"Three times," Laura whispered, waiting for her to say more.

With her back to Laura, Mikatrin said, "It's what you wanted, isn't it? It's the life you wanted."

Laura held out her hands to show her daughter the tadpole: a gift, a vision. Annile wanted to drink from her cupped palms.

"No, he'll jump out," Laura said, but she tilted her hands toward the small red mouth. The tadpole leapt frantically, striking the startled child in the cheek, and fell back into the spring.

The water rippled and danced; Laura saw her reflection shift. She looked into the water and watched it draw the picture of a younger woman, a woman in a dark green dress edged with white lace at the throat, her hair long and glossy and well kept, her hands smooth and white, her nails clean and even.

"Who's that?" her daughter asked, following her mother's gaze, wanting to play this old game, to hear her mother's dreams.

"Why, that's a young woman I know," Laura answered. "A teacher."

"Tell me about her, Mama."

She pulled the child up closer to her on the log, cast an eye at the baby digging in the mud. "Well, let's see. She's just started teaching. She found a little apartment all to herself with a view of the Three Sisters, way off. Sometimes she just reads away the evenings in a big comfortable chair. She likes to sew, she sewed that dress to wear to a dance. Her beau comes on Friday nights in a dark gray suit and sometimes they go out to eat. Once in a while she takes a trip. Greece, to swim in the sea."

Annile thought for a good time.

"Have you ever been there?"

"No, I haven't. Bought a book about Greece, though. I gave it to your great-great-aunt Johanna when I was a girl."

"Is the teacher lady you?"

Laura stroked the child's hair away from her face and looked back into the depths of the spring.

"No, that was never me. But maybe it'll be you, sometime. Maybe you can take up where your great-aunt Martha left off. She was a fine teacher."

"Gran says I'll be a farmer's wife," Annile volunteered.

Mikatrin.

I never took off and left a kitchen full of work to be done, Laura imagined Mikatrin saying.

But they're little for such a short time, she answered, even as she gathered her children to her to start back.

The day ebbed, but they walked slowly. At the turn of the path where it left the woods, Laura hesitated. Annile sat down in a patch of wildflowers, spotty now as the summer wore away. Laura looked at the Three Sisters, the meadows, the busy expanse of their small homestead, an oasis in an eternity of trees and hills, green layer upon layer in shades of the coming night. And in the shadows lengthening on the vegetable garden she saw children playing: the child she had lost, grown sturdy and up to mischief, peeking out from leafy corners in an endless game of hide-and-seek; the other children she would bear or lose before she was forty; the grandchildren who would come soon after.

From this good distance Laura watched Martin as he loaded the cans, now filled with fresh milk, onto the tractor to take them down to the stand for pickup. She knew that he was ticking off chores to himself, counting the time until he could put aside the work and come in to the house to sit with her in the circle of light in the kitchen.

If only he would look up, he would see them there, watching him.

He bent over the tractor hitch.

I wish my mother had took us walking in the evening, she imagined him saying.

So do I, she answered him.

And a sea of wanting him washed over her, left her shaking: he must come looking for her, he must put his arms around her and see what she saw. Laura wanted him to climb the path to them in his long, quick stride; she saw him smiling, reaching out to take their sleeping, muddy boy, pausing to run a hand over the growing curve of her belly.

Let me, she heard him say. *Rest your arms.*

And: *Tomorrow we'll just go see about a new wedding ring.*

What about the hay? she asked him.

It can wait, he said.

After a time, she knew that it could not, that he could not, and she shook herself, and went down to him.

Clan Charts

The three charts that follow show the family relationships of the people chronicled in *Homestead*. Legal names appear inside the boxes, clan names outside in italics; an asterisk indicates that the person also appears in another clan chart.

ℬengat Clan

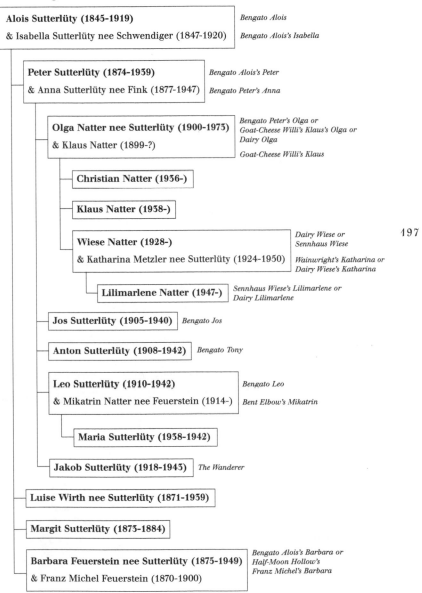

Alois Sutterlüty (1845-1919)
& Isabella Sutterlüty nee Schwendiger (1847-1920)

Bengato Alois
Bengato Alois's Isabella

Peter Sutterlüty (1874-1939)
& Anna Sutterlüty nee Fink (1877-1947)

Bengato Alois's Peter
Bengato Peter's Anna

Olga Natter nee Sutterlüty (1900-1973)
& Klaus Natter (1899-?)

Bengato Peter's Olga or
Goat-Cheese Willi's Klaus's Olga or
Dairy Olga

Goat-Cheese Willi's Klaus

Christian Natter (1936-)

Klaus Natter (1938-)

Wiese Natter (1928-)
& Katharina Metzler nee Sutterlüty (1924-1950)

Dairy Wiese or
Sennhaus Wiese

Wainwright's Katharina or
Dairy Wiese's Katharina

197

Lilimarlene Natter (1947-)

Sennhaus Wiese's Lilimarlene or
Dairy Lilimarlene

Jos Sutterlüty (1905-1940) *Bengato Jos*

Anton Sutterlüty (1908-1942) *Bengato Tony*

Leo Sutterlüty (1910-1942)
& Mikatrin Natter nee Feuerstein (1914-)

Bengato Leo
Bent Elbow's Mikatrin

Maria Sutterlüty (1938-1942)

Jakob Sutterlüty (1918-1943) *The Wanderer*

Luise Wirth nee Sutterlüty (1871-1939)

Margit Sutterlüty (1873-1884)

Barbara Feuerstein nee Sutterlüty (1875-1949)
& Franz Michel Feuerstein (1870-1900)

Bengato Alois's Barbara or
Half-Moon Hollow's
Franz Michel's Barbara

Bent Elbow Clan

Sefftone Lang (1850-1903)
& Rita Lang nee Troy (1854-1890)

Angelika Feuerstein nee Lang (1885-1938)
& Hans Feuerstein (1884-1936)

Bent Elbow's Angelika

Hans from the Hill or
Bent Elbow's Hans

Bent Elbow's Mikatrin*

Mikatrin Sutterlüty nee Feuerstein (1914-)
& (1) Leo Sutterlüty (1910-1942)

Maria (1938-1942)

Bengato Peter's Leo*

& (2) Martin Schwendiger (1916-)

Cobbler's Youngest or
Cobbler's Martin

Rudi (1948-)

Kaspar (1950-)
Jok (1950-)

Markus (1949-)

Martin Schwendiger the Younger (1947-)
& Laura Schwendiger nee Ritter (1950-)

Bent Elbow's Martin

Kasparle's Laura or
Bent Elbow Martin's Laura

Jakob (1975-)

Annile (1972-)

Martha Feuerstein (1917-1973)

Bent Elbow's Martha or
Miss Martha

Johanna Lang (1879-1975)
& Francesco Donati (1870-?)

Bent Elbow's Johanna or
Hanna

The Wainwright's Clan

Jos Metzler

& Maria Ursula Metzler nee Metzler

The Wainwright

Ignaz Metzler (1852-1945)

& (1) **Annakatrina Metzler nee Greber** (1845-1890)   *Old Woman*

Richard Metzler (1878-1902)   *Wainwright's Richard*

& Rosa Metzler nee Fink (1880-1901)   *River's Bend Rosa or Wainwright's Rosa*

Stante Metzler (1901-)   *Wainwright's Stante*

Michel Metzler (1901-1938)

Marie Metzler (1879-1980)   *Wainwright's Marie or Grumpy Marie or The Postmistress*

& (2) **Theres Metzler nee Bischof** (1897-1952)   *Miller's Theres or Wainwright's Theres*

Wainwright's Katharina or Sennhaus Wiese's Katharina*

Katharina Metzler (1924-1950)

& (1) Ahmed

The Moroccan

Lilimarlene Natter (1947-)

Dairy or Sennhaus Lilimarlene*

& (2) Wiese Natter (1928-)   *Dairy or Sennhaus Wiese**

199

Naming Conventions

In addition to a legal last name, most persons in these villages of Vorarlberg are also known by a *Hausname*, or clan name. This convention has arisen because there are a dozen or fewer family names that recur in the villages, and many extremely common first names, especially in the older generation. Throughout this book, clan names have been anglicized where possible for the sake of clarity; for instance, Goat-Cheese Willi's Klaus for the (fictional) original *Goßkäs Willis Klaus*, Dairy Alois for *Sennhus Alois*, and so forth.

Clan names are not static but change and evolve over time. They are of three basic types:

1. A dominant family personality, usually but not always a man, serves as a focal point for the whole clan: *Kasparles Laura, Annobüoblis Rudolf, Kolobano Kaspars Kaspar.* This type of clan name can become very complex: *Dokwieses Aloiso Peters Maria,* which would commonly be understood from right to left: Maria, married to (or daughter of) Peter, son of Alois, son of Dokwiese.

2. A family profession or skill serves as identification: *Sennhus* (or Dairy) *Katharina* (Katharina of the dairy master's clan); *Adlarweorts Hedwig* (Hedwig, of the Eagle Innkeeper's clan).

3. The family's homestead location gives the clan its name: *Bengato Alois*; *Ellaboga Johanna* (Bent Elbow's Johanna).

Sometimes more than one of these conventions is used: *Bengato Peters Anna*, which would be understood as Anna, wife (or daughter) of Peter of the Bengat homestead; *Saddlars Antons Marikatrin*, which would be understood as Marikatrin, wife (or daughter) of Anton of the saddle-maker's clan, and would be used if there is more than one branch of the saddlers. When women leave the family home to marry, they usually come to be called by a new clan name, most often that of the husband.

First names are often varied by joining two together: Mikatrin (Maria Katharina), Kasparnazi (Kaspar Ignaz). The suffix *-le*, from written German *-lein*, is a diminutive and usually an affectionate one: Sefftonile (Little Josef Anton).

Pronunciation Guide

Characters and place names, in the High Alemannic dialect of the village:

Alois	Áh-loh-wees
Angelika	Ahn-géy-lee-kah
Anna	Ah-nah
Annamarile	Ah-nah-mah-rée-leh
Annile	Áh-neh-leh
Annobüobli	Áhna-bü-ah-b-leh
Anton	Áhn-tone
(Tonile)	(Toh-neh-leh)
Barbara	Báh-rr-bah-rah
(Bärbele)	(Bär-beh-leh)
Bartle	Bah-rt-leh
Bengat	Behn-gáht
Christian	Khrrisch-tschahn
Däta	Deh-tah
Francesco	F-rahn-chase-coh

Gide	Gée-deh
Hans	Hah-ns
Ignaz	Ig-nahtz
Isabella	Is-ah-béll-ah
Jakob	Yáh-kohb
Jodok	Yoh-dohk
Johanna	Yo-háh-nah
Jok	Yohk
Jos	Yohs
Kaspar	Káhsch-pahr
Katharina	Kah-tah-réen-ah
Klaus	K-l-ah-oos
Konstantin	Kóhn-schtahn-teen
(Stante)	(Schtáhn-teh)
Laura	Lah-ow-rah
Lilimarlene	Lil-ee-mahrr-léh-neh
Martha	Mah-rr-tah
Martin	Mahrr-teen
Michel	Mih-chel
Mikatrin	Mée-kah-trreen
Olga	Owl-gah
Peter	Peh-tehrr
Rosenau	Roh-sehn-ah-o
Rudi	Rood-ee
Sennhus	Sehnn-hoos
Theres	Teh-raise
Willi	Vill-ee

Glossary

Alp. Living accommodations at the higher altitudes occupied only at the height of the summer for about a two-month period. Cattle are generally driven to alp directly from *Vorschaß* in order to take advantage of meadows that cannot be hayed. This is often a communal undertaking; a group of farmers hire an alpler, usually a young man trained in making cheese–although some alps are dedicated solely to yearlings and there is no cheese production. The term "alp" is not used as a synonym for "mountain."

Fasching. Mardi Gras, the season of masked balls, dances, and fairs before Lent.

Gada. The main bedroom of the farmhouse, belonging to the parents.

Heimatabend. Concert in which local music and dancing, to some degree contrived for the purpose, is demonstrated for tourists.

Jass. A regional card game played with a distinctive set of cards in four suits.

Juppa. Before the First World War, the common name for the dress type worn by the farm women of the Bregenz Forest; usually black, finely pleated and starched, with a bodice, worn on workdays with dark underblouse and blue, often patterned apron (with a less somber Sunday and holiday version). After the war the *Juppa* was gradually supplanted by a wider variety of "outsider" fashions. Today it is worn primarily on holidays and Sundays and not by all women.

Kilbe. Anniversary of churches consecrated to Saints Peter and Paul; parish festival (*Kirchweihfest* in written German).

Schopf. A covered, partially enclosed gallery usually two stories high. On the north or west side of old farmhouses there is always a *Schopf*. The main entrance of the house is accessed through this gallery, where the family often eats and sits in the evening in warm weather. It is the site of a wide variety of activities, from needlework to courting. The windows on the upper level are sometimes cut in fanciful shapes; the window-like openings on the lower level can be shuttered against the weather.

Sennhaus. A dairy or any cheese-making facility, but more recently a centralized communal dairy specializing in the local cheese.

Stadel. The storage and general work area that links the farmhouse with the barn and cowshed.

Stopfar. White cornmeal fried in butterfat, eaten from a communal frying pan, usually by dipping each spoonful into a cup of milk or coffee. *Stopfar* is very common breakfast food, but is sometimes eaten in the evening as well.

Stube. A sitting room, the main room of the house.

Vorschaß. A general term for the living arrangements at a higher altitude where the family goes to stay for a period of weeks in the spring and again in the fall so that the livestock can graze the mountain pastures, leaving the valley fields and pastures for haying (in written German, usually *Voralpe*).

Acknowledgments

I owe a very large debt to the women of the Bregenz Forest who have shared their life stories with me so freely for the past twenty years. In particular I would like to thank the women of two families for making me feel at home in their villages: in Großdorf, the Wiar women—Rosa and Martha, and their mother, Laura; and the *Sennhus* women in Andelsbuch—Olga and her daughters, Maria, Katharina, Elisabeth, Margit, and especially Rita. Finally, my dearest wish, but an impossible one, is to make Marlies Nenning understand what her friendship and generosity have meant to me these many years.

These stories could not have been written if it were not for the apparently inexhaustible support of my friends: Emmy Liston, Marty Calvert, Janet Gilsdorf, Gene Case, Amy Czarnecki, and David Karraker. I am especially grateful to Rosellen Brown and Charlie Baxter for providing words of encouragement when they were most needed.

I am thankful to my agent, Jill Grinberg, for her tenacious faith in these stories, and for bringing them to the attention of

Joy Johannessen at Delphinium. Each and every sentence seems to hum a little truer because of Joy's perfect pitch. I am very fortunate to have had her guidance and help in the last stage of the creation of this book.

Finally, I continue to depend on Bill for his rock-solid faith in me, and on Elisabeth, who has taught me to have faith in myself.